SOUTHERN CONJURING

SWEET TEA WITCH MYSTERIES BOOK THIRTEEN

AMY BOYLES

LADYBUGBOOKS LLC

ONE

"Oh, so you're the culprit with the mason jars."

I'd come down to the kitchen for a glass of sweet tea and found the living room filled to the brim with boxes of mason jars. I'd thought that was strange enough, but when I entered the kitchen, that's when I discovered my cousin Amelia sitting at the table in front of even more boxes of dusty and grimy jars.

She tugged at her blonde hair. The pixie cut that I'd known Amelia to have since, well ever since I'd met her, was slowly growing out. Soft blonde curls sprouted, haloing her face.

She released a shot of air. "They were shipped to the Vault from someone looking to get rid of them. Erasmus Everlasting asked me to bring them home and dust them."

"All of them?" I asked, incredulous.

She nodded. "All of them."

I stared at the box of seemingly harmless glassware. "Why would he have you dust it here if it's supposed to go in the Vault?"

The Vault was Magnolia Cove's storage unit for all objects magical.

Amelia shrugged. "I don't really know. They're supposed to separate things, but they must not be dangerous if Erasmus is letting them out of the Vault. Besides, we're overrun with objects right now. He's got to reorganize things to create more space."

I frowned. "We're magical. Can't he just use a spell and make the Vault bigger?"

"You would think." Amelia raked her fingers down her tired face. "But apparently it's not that simple."

"Nothing ever is in Magnolia Cove." I opened the fridge. "Just be careful. I don't want something bad happening to us."

The kitchen door opened, and my grandmother, Betty Craple, strolled in wearing a floral dress, white gloves and a white hat.

"You having tea with the queen?" I said.

Amelia giggled. "You are fancy."

Betty glared daggers of fire at us.

"You do look nice," I said quickly. "I didn't mean the tea thing in a bad way."

Betty pulled a pipe from her pocket and shoved it between her teeth. "This better? Now I don't look like I'm having tea with anyone, do I?"

Amelia and I exchanged a look. "No, you still look like you're having tea with someone."

Betty snarled.

"Well, with an attitude like that, no one's going to want to have tea with you," Amelia said.

I stifled a laugh.

"For your information," Betty snorted, "I have a meeting of the Magnolia Cove Founding Witches. We don't meet that often, and when we do, I have to dress up."

Amelia arched a brow. "Is that because Snow Wigley's going to be there?"

I hiked a brow. "Snow Wigley? Who's that?"

Betty frowned. "Don't you be worrying about Snow Wigley."

"Snow," Amelia informed me, "is only Betty's oldest rival when it comes to who has the best and most successful life."

I scoffed. "If it weren't for Betty, Magnolia Cove wouldn't even exist."

They stared at me blankly.

"Okay, maybe the town would exist, but Betty's the witch connected to the heart stone. If the heart stone didn't have anyone connected to it, the town's magic would go kaput."

The heart stone was an actual stone made from a heart that lived in our fireplace. Yes, it sounds weird, I know, but just roll with it.

All of Magnolia Cove's magic is tied to that stone, and the stone, in turn, is tied to a living person—my grandmother.

Betty scratched her bald scalp underneath the curly gray wig she wore. "That's true, but my rivalry with Snow goes way back. For several years her daughter was Magical Ambassador to Britain."

I cringed. "Oh, and your daughters—"

The back door opened abruptly, slamming against the wall. Mint and Licky Craple, my aunts and Betty's children, strolled inside, wide smiles on their faces.

I went ahead and finished my sentence to Betty. "Your daughters are chaos witches."

"You see how Snow wins," Betty said.

I flashed my engagement ring at her. "Well, I just got engaged to a man who pretty much single-handedly stopped a werewolf/witch fight in the South. If that's not enough, I defeated Lacy the Evil, as I like to refer to her, in a witch match that was almost to the death."

"Your death," Amelia said.

That was all true. A couple of weeks ago the Head Witch Order had arrived with one purpose—to steal my powers. I could either go with them willingly or have my magic sucked from me.

I chose neither.

Luckily it all worked out and I defeated their leader, Lacy.

In the end, everything had turned out okay. Amelia even got a new sweetie out of the deal—Sherman Oaks, a bumbling wizard but one that practically worshipped the ground Amelia walked on.

If you asked me, that was what she needed. Before Sherman, Amelia hadn't had much luck with men.

But anyway, Mint and Licky had arrived, and all our attention was honed on the two chaos witches.

Betty cocked her chin at them. "What do you two want?"

So much for a welcome greeting.

Mint raked her finger through her silky locks. "We only came over to say hello."

"And we're sorry we missed the Head Witch Order," Licky added, twisting a few strands of her straight hair into a braid. "But there were things we had to do."

"Or we would've been here to fight," Mint said proudly. "But as it was—"

"We were on vacation," Licky finished.

"Good thing," Betty said. "Now, what is it you want?"

Mint and Licky exchanged a smile. Mint spoke. "We've come to escort you to the Magnolia Cove Founding Witches meeting."

She raised one fisted hand and snapped her wrist. Flames unfurled in the air, revealing a sheet of pristine white paper.

Betty paled. "What in tarnation is that?"

Mint smiled. "It's our invitation to join the club."

"We are descendants of the people who started this town," Licky said.

"So naturally we'd eventually be asked to join."

The veins in Betty's temples popped. "No. Absolutely not. There is no way y'all two are going to the meeting and embarrassing me."

Mint's mouth dropped open in shock. She splayed a hand over her chest. "Mama, we just want to go and support you."

Betty ignored her. "Oh, Snow will have a field day with this. She probably sent you the invitations, knowing what it'll do to me that you'll be there. She'll be spouting off about her daughter the ex-ambassador, and I'll be explaining how my daughters nearly destroy anything they come in contact with."

Licky folded her arms and said crossly, "I take offense to that sort of talk."

"You can take offense all you want, but that's how it is." Betty's gaze swept around the room until it landed on me and Amelia. "Y'all two, pack up. If Mint and Licky are going to the meeting, so are y'all."

I shot Amelia a confused look. "But we weren't invited."

"I'll say you're my guests." Betty's gaze landed on the mason jars. "What are those?"

Amelia opened her mouth to answer.

"Never mind, bring those too," Betty commanded. "We're all going." She eyed my outfit of jeans and a T-shirt. "That won't do."

My grandmother snapped her fingers, and I was suddenly draped in a violet suit dress. Double-breasted buttons lined the jacket, and the cuffs flared just slightly. I touched my head and found Betty had topped off the outfit with a hat.

My gaze landed on Amelia, and she looked exactly the same, except she wore powder blue. "Is it okay if I finish cleaning the jars."

Betty sniffed. "If you must, but sit in the back."

I frowned. "Won't that look weird? Amelia cleaning?"

Betty shook her head. "They'll think she's the help. It'll be fine."

Amelia's face fell. "That's not an insult or anything."

Betty shooed us toward the door. "I'll tell them you're doing official Vault business. That'll twist up Snow's girdle good and tight. No one will question you after that."

I shot Amelia a hopeful look. "I'm game if you are."

Amelia shook her head. "You haven't met Snow. Once you meet her, you'll wish you'd never gone."

Mint clapped her hands. "Is everyone ready? I'll whisk us there by magic."

"I'll take care of myself and my granddaughters," Betty snapped. "There's no telling where you'll end up sending us if we go with y'all."

Licky brushed a bit of lint from her shoulders. "Well then, we'll see y'all there."

My aunts clapped their hands in unison, and in less than a blink they'd vanished.

"Let's just hope they end up in Bermuda and I don't have to deal with it," Betty said. She opened the door and stared outside. "Are the two of y'all ready?"

Amelia grabbed the box of rattling mason jars. "I feel like such an idiot."

"But at least you're an idiot with style," I said. "Besides, wouldn't you rather be entertained by your mom and aunt instead of sitting here cleaning jars all alone?"

Amelia shrugged. "That's a hard call."

"Buck up, kids," Betty said. "Tighten your hats, hold on to your panties and let's get ready to attend this meeting. There's no time for cast-iron skillet riding. We're doing this the old-fashioned way—by magic."

"Isn't everything in this town done by magic?"

Betty shot me a scathing look. "Don't go getting smart on me, girl. I'm too old to put up with that crap."

"Sorry," I said.

Betty lit her corncob pipe and covered one nostril. A tendril of sparkling magic swirled from her nose and surrounded us. "Here we go," she said.

The magic coiled, engulfing me. The backyard faded away, and a moment later I was standing on a cliff overlooking a deep bluff. A raging river gushed below.

I felt some sort of invisible force pulling me forward before a hand clutched the scruff of my neck and yanked me back.

"Turn around, kid," Betty said. "We're here."

I pressed a hand to my chest. My heart beat frantically, pounding all the way into my ears.

I pivoted to find the three of us standing in front of a blue cottage tucked into a forest, overlooking the bluff.

"Where are we? I thought you said we were in Magnolia Cove."

Betty adjusted her hat low, nearly covering her eyes. "We're in the Cobweb Forest."

"Who lives *here*?" I said, unbelieving. The Cobweb Forest could be a dangerous place—moving trees, unknown creatures, possibly giant spiders. I just made up the last one, but you never knew. No one lived out here. No one.

At least until now.

Amelia adjusted the box in her arms. "Snow Wigley, that's who."

I stared at the cottage. A round porthole window sat at the very top of what appeared to be the third floor. A shadow moved across the glass and light flickered.

Chill bumps rushed down my spine. The cottage was a cheery blue with white lacy trim. It looked inviting, but at the same time there was something eerie about it.

I felt like I was standing at the mouth of the witch's home in "Hansel and Gretel." If I wasn't careful, I'd be tossed into a fire.

The front door creaked open.

Amelia shuddered. "This is so creepy. How long do we have to stay?"

Betty's chin stiffened. "As long as it takes or until your mother embarrasses us."

A woman who looked to be in her midsixties stood in the doorframe. She wore a snow-white antebellum dress, ringlet curls and dark eyeliner that made her look at least one hundred years old as well as crazy.

"Whoa," I whispered. "Who invited Baby Jane?" I referenced the old movie *Whatever Happened to Baby Jane?*

Amelia ribbed me. I sucked air, and then suddenly realized exactly who I was looking at.

Snow Wigley stretched out her arms and, in the most caustic voice ever—seriously, it sounded like her vocal cords had been raked over gravel—she said, "Betty Craple, welcome to my home. Your daughters are already here, ready to be initiated into the group. I see you've brought your granddaughters. Come in, young ladies. Come in."

Her gaze darted to the trees. "Hurry, you never know what lurks in this forest. You'd better come inside before the family of rabid possums that's been living under the bluffs decides to jump up and attack."

Amelia's voice shook with fear. "Rabid possums?"

Snow cackled, a true witch's cackle. Betty snaked her hands through our arms, linking us. "Come on, girls. Let's go. Better get out of the open before something happens."

Snow smiled and gestured for us to enter. The stairs creaked as I ascended the porch. "Come in."

The old witch gave us room to sweep past her. "This should be enjoyable," Snow said. "Mint and Licky Craple are about to cast a spell to see if they're ready to join."

Betty snarled. "What sort of spell?"

Snow's eyes glittered with delight. "Why, a conjuring spell, of course. Mint and Licky are about to conjure a spirit from the other side." She leaned forward. "Let's hope they get it right."

Her tone made me feel like a sliver of ice was running down my back. "Why's that?"

"Because, dear," Snow said as if I were a simple girl who could barely understand American English, "if they conjure an evil spirit, that could kill us all."

Snow smiled widely as she shut the door behind us, closing us in.

TWO

$\mathcal{W}$e didn't get a round of welcomes like I would have expected. A dozen or so witches dotted Snow's living room. They held punch glasses and sipped from elegant crystal as they waited for the show to begin.

I recognized several of them. Saltz Swift from the Southern School of Magic sipped a cocktail. He smoothed his slicked-back hair and cocked an appreciative eyebrow at me.

My gaze darted to the person standing next to him. Sylvia Spirits, a tall red-haired woman wearing a flowing red dress, smiled at me. She lifted her glass in hello.

I smiled and nodded.

Sylvia was great. A powerful witch who owned Charming Conical Caps and a woman who worked to keep Magnolia Cove safe.

"Love your cap," Amelia said.

Sylvia touched the pointed golden hat atop her head. "This old thing? It's a memory hat. Keeps all my memories so that I can watch them later. Like watching a movie."

I gave the hat an admiring look. "It's beautiful."

"Hey there, Miss Dunn."

I glanced over to see CJ Hix smiling goofily at me. I shot him a big grin.

"Hey, CJ, good to see you."

He elbowed me gently. "You here to join the club?"

I laughed and shook my head. "No, not at all. I'm here to make sure Mint and Licky don't burn the place down."

CJ swatted the air playfully. "Oh, Snow would never allow that. There's nothing to worry about."

An older man standing nearby narrowed his eyes at CJ. CJ noticed. He laughed nervously and turned to me. "Well, it appears I've been summoned by Forbes Henry."

That must've been the old man. "I'm afraid I don't know him."

CJ smirked. "Forbes Henry is old, rich and thinks he owns the place."

"Sure he's not related to Betty?" Amelia said.

CJ chuckled good-naturedly. "No, I don't believe that. But I think Mr. Henry has a property he'd like me to list. He wanted to discuss it."

"How's your business going?" I asked. Last time I'd seen CJ, he'd listed a property of a man who was assumed to be dead but in fact was not.

Yes, very strange happenings in Magnolia Cove.

CJ ran his fingers through his hair. "Oh, it's just dandy. Keeps me busy."

Forbes shot CJ another cold look. "But I guess I'd better be going."

"Yeah, don't get in trouble," Amelia whispered.

I said goodbye, and CJ strode off to speak to the older man.

"I wonder what that was all about," Amelia said.

There wasn't time to question it because Snow clapped her hands. The conversations died down. "I believe we're all here. It's time for the Proof of Craft."

We joined Betty in a corner. Amelia placed the box of rattling mason jars on a buffet. "Are you going to let them do this?"

Betty shrugged. "What choice do I have?"

My cousin watched the scene unfold. "They'll probably open a vortex straight to the underworld."

Betty shrugged. "There are plenty of witches here who could close it."

"These witches don't look like they're interested in anything other than the punch," I murmured.

Mint and Licky took positions on either side of a cauldron of bubbling green liquid.

They chanted low, but I could still make out the words. "Who are they conjuring?" I directed to Betty.

"Sounds like a spirit that cleans the house."

I shot her a skeptical look. "You're kidding."

She shook her head. "I'm not. Listen."

My aunts said the words together. *"Sprite of light, sprite of might, make my house clean and bright."*

They each threw a handful of ingredients into the cauldron. A plume of yellow sulfuric smoke rose to the ceiling, and a second later a white, cloud-like spirit stood in the middle of the room.

"What is it you command of me?" the spirit said.

Mint and Licky looked to Snow for approval. The room erupted into clapping. Snow flicked her hand as if to dismiss the spirit.

Mint nodded. "You may leave, spirit. Thank you for your help."

"Hmm," I murmured. "I wonder if that spirit could help me do some cleaning."

"Don't even think about it," Betty snarled. "You need to do things the old-fashioned way. Taking shortcuts is never a good idea."

"Well, it sounded good to me," I said.

"I'm shocked they didn't kill anyone," Amelia said. "It's not even Christmas, the time for miracles."

I snorted. The room's clapping dissolved, and Snow announced that Mint and Licky would be the newest members of the Magnolia Cove Founding Witches group.

About an hour later the meeting was over and people were congratulating Mint and Licky on a job well done.

I wandered around the room, eyeing the antiques that Snow had accumulated. I placed a hand on a silver jewelry box.

"It's a very pretty piece."

My gaze flickered to Snow, who stood beside me like a shadow. I moved away to give myself some personal space. "It is."

Snow lifted it from the table. Delicate silver filigree curled around the sides. "The funny thing about this box is that the spirit trapped inside it fought so hard when I made him enter. He didn't seem to understand that I wanted him for my own personal collection."

My eyelids flared. "I'm sorry? You trapped a spirit?"

"Yes." Snow gestured around the room. "These were all troublesome spirits or sprites, little pestering fairies that needed to be dealt with. Some had wreaked havoc on witches. One in particular believed it was his life's duty to turn all witch's hair the color green."

"Ew," I said.

"Yes. Ew." She moved closer. She flicked a hand toward a leather-bound book on a shelf. "And that's my pride and joy there—a book filled with creatures. I would say it's the most complete compilation of magical species that ever existed."

I peered at the golden letters running down the binding. "*Catchings and Conjurings of Creatures Mythical.*" I quirked a brow. "Catchings of them?"

Snow nodded. "Yes, it's quite unique. It houses everything from magic eaters to trolls." She dragged her gaze from the book back to me. "I saw the look of interest when your aunts worked their spell. Are you interested in conjuring, Pepper Dunn?"

My mouth quirked. I was sort of interested in conjuring, I guessed. "If I can make a cleaning spirit show up and go through my closet, that would be great. I would love that."

As if on cue, Snow pulled a slip of paper from her pocket. "These are the instructions if you decide to do it. It's very simple, and when you want the spirit to return to the other side, just tell it to go and it will. You saw how we did it."

I swallowed a knot in my throat. "I did. I saw."

She smiled widely. "Then you know it's simple."

"Simple," I repeated dumbly. "Very simple. But I don't know…"

Snow inhaled and her chest rose proudly. "Pepper Dunn, you are the strongest witch that Magnolia Cove may have ever seen. To not know how to conjure is a travesty. Conjuring is your right as a witch. You may need that talent sometime." She nodded toward the paper. "I suggest you take it."

Then as if Snow was the devil whispering into one of my ears and Betty was an angel on the other, my grandmother sidled up beside me, her hands on her hips. "You ready to go, Pepper?"

I clutched the paper tightly. The last thing I wanted was for Betty to see me taking something from Snow. She'd be so angry her eyes might explode from her head.

"Yes, I'm ready. Never been more ready. Wow, I am *super* ready."

Betty peered at me as if studying every curve of my face. "You're talking like you're nervous."

I waved away her concern. "I'm not nervous. Wow. Where has the time gone? I need to help Amelia clean up those mason jars."

I glanced at Snow. Mischief sparkled in her eyes. I understood her point—conjuring was part of a witch's arsenal—but I didn't feel I was ready for that.

I didn't want a conjuring spell. Why would I need it? I grasped Snow's hands and tucked the slip of paper back in them.

I swished past Betty, grabbed the box of mason jars and headed to the door. Amelia eyed me like I'd lost my mind.

"You okay?"

I nodded. "Snow tried to give me the conjuring spell that Mint and Licky used."

"Betty would kill her if she found out."

I nodded. "I know."

While Betty said goodbye to Snow, Amelia studied me. "So'd you give the spell back to her?"

I nodded. "Yeah, I don't need any of that nonsense."

Amelia *tsked.*

"What?"

"Oh, I don't know," she said innocently. "There's a lot more mason jars to clean after I'm done with these."

I scoffed. "I thought you said I shouldn't take it?"

Amelia tipped her head to the side. "I only said Betty would kill someone. I didn't say it was a bad idea. In fact, I think having a cleaning spirit would come in handy every once in a while. Like now." She gestured toward the jars. "I only have one box with me, but the witch who donated them to the Vault gave us a truckload."

A spike of excitement ran down my spine before I tamped it back down. "I guess you'll just have to wash them the old-fashioned way."

"Fine," Amelia huffed.

Betty marched toward us. "Girls, let's get out of here. I'm afraid if we stay too long in this forest, something bad might happen."

Amelia took the box from me. "What sort of bad?"

"Snow might convince you she's a decent person." Betty cocked an eye at me. "Like she did to you."

Unbelievable. "Let's get out of here, shall we?" We stepped onto the porch. A breeze picked up the hair on the back of my neck. "What about Mint and Licky?"

"They're going to stay with Snow for a while." Betty rolled her eyes. "Learn some of the secrets of the group."

"Do you have secrets?" Amelia asked.

"No," Betty snapped. "The only secret is that for the most part we're a bunch of old people."

I bit back a laugh. We headed down the porch and started toward the spot where we'd arrived.

A scratching from underneath the house caught my attention. I brushed away a strand of hair the wind had whipped into my eyes and peered toward the latticework that covered the crawl space.

"What is that?"

"Probably those rabid possums Snow told us about," Betty said smartly.

I was skeptical. I didn't really believe that a family of rabid possums lived near the house.

But the scratching continued. "Something might be caught down there."

I peered between the lattice. Darkness greeted me. I made out cobwebs, thick wooden beams and a dirt floor. "I guess it was nothing."

Just then something hit the side of the crawl space, bouncing off the wooden barrier.

I screamed and shot away from the house. My heart thundered. Blood pounded in my ears. "What was that?"

"Come closer."

Amelia appeared beside me. "Oh my gosh, the house is talking."

"It wasn't the house," Betty said. "It was a creature underneath it."

"The rabid possum," Amelia shrieked.

A face appeared from behind the lattice. White fur, a brown nose and glittering black eyes stared at us.

"I'm not rabid," it said in a raspy voice that reminded me more of the serpent in the Garden of Eden tempting Eve than a possum. "Please. Let me out."

I looked to Betty for guidance on this one. I didn't know if the possum was rabid, but I was pretty certain if it got in there by itself, it should be able to get out.

Plus, it was speaking where all three of us could hear it. It wasn't just an animal talking in my head. No, this sucker spoke American.

"Why should we let you out?" I said.

Its little paw reached through the barrier, palm up. It was so cute and human. "She tricked me and put me here. That woman. Please, I'm not really a possum."

Amelia and I glanced at Betty. "If you're not really a possum, then Snow had a reason for whatever she did. Besides, there's no way for us to know if you're lying. You could be a murderer that she imprisoned."

"I'm not a murderer," the possum said. "Just lonely."

Amelia adjusted the box in her hands until it rested on her hip. "Well in that case, my name's Amelia and this is Pepper. We're cousins. Pepper is sort of my long-lost cousin, but ever since we met we've become really close. We have another cousin, Cordelia. She's temperamental and makes smart remarks all the time, but deep down she's a kitten. Anyway, I don't currently have a boyfriend—"

I cleared my throat, interrupting her. "That's not true. You have a kinda boyfriend."

Amelia nodded. "Sherman Oaks is my kinda boyfriend. We're just getting to know each other. Sherman doesn't live here, but he visits often. Pepper here just got engaged."

"Why don't you tell the possum what you had for breakfast," Betty snarked.

Amelia ignored her. "As I was saying, Pepper just got engaged and is currently planning her wedding."

"I could help you," the possum said. "I know about weddings. I've seen ant wedding ceremonies. It can't be too different."

How to politely say I thought that yes, those would be very different?

"Um, thanks," I said kindly. "But what I'm looking to do isn't similar."

Betty pushed her pipe between her teeth and jutted out her chin. "Come on, girls. Let's go."

We walked away from the possum, but I couldn't help feeling a twinge of sadness. Surely there was a reason for this little guy to be there.

It wasn't any of my business, right? None of it.

We left the possum behind, but something bothered me. I got one last look at the furry little face before Betty whisked us back home— back to a house filled with mason jars.

THREE

"*I*'m going out for an hour, and when I come back, I want these mason jars gone."

Betty stood with legs splayed wide. She stared at the mountains of glass that lined every single wall and were scattered across the floor in the house.

"I'm giving you an hour," she snapped. "Have them gone, or when I get back, I'll vanish all of them to the ocean."

Amelia's eyes widened. "You can't do that. This is my job on the line."

Betty *humphed*. "I don't care about your job. I care about finding my house."

With that, she left, slamming the door behind her. I shot a look to Amelia. "Looks like you'd better get to cleaning."

The back door opened. That would be Cordelia returning home from work. One, two, three...

"What in the world is going on here? Amelia! I know this is your doing!"

Cordelia stormed into the living room, flames shooting from her eyes. "What is going on?"

My phone buzzed as Amelia started to explain the predicament. I glanced at the number and sighed happily.

"Hey there," I answered in a husky voice.

"Hey, yourself," Axel answered. "How's my favorite lady doing?"

I giggled. "I'm doing great, though I'm trying to avoid the apocalypse here at the house."

"Is Betty involved?" he joked.

"No, but Amelia and Cordelia are."

"Then you'd better get out now."

I laughed and pressed my ear closer to the phone. It was so good to hear Axel's voice. I hadn't talked to him all day, and my heart shuddered in misery at how much I missed him.

"Want to get dinner tonight?"

"Yes, because I want to talk to you about venue locations for the wedding."

He sighed. Axel had already put up with me going over at least five places. He said he didn't care where we got married, but I wanted the location to be perfect.

"Why don't we have the wedding at your house?" he said, which I took as he wanted to keep everything very, very simple. Plus, to be honest, I think he was tired of me showing him different venues.

I balked. "At Betty's? Well, for one it's too small."

He laughed. I didn't have to see Axel to know he was throwing his head back as a big belly chuckle flowed through him. "This is a town of witches. Size means nothing to us."

I nibbled my bottom lip. "I don't know. I feel like having it here would be asking for disaster."

His voice lowered. "Whatever you say. If you want to discuss wedding venues over barbecue, that's fine with me."

"Good." Cordelia and Amelia's argument seemed to be heating up. Amelia's face had reddened, and Cordelia was waving her arms around. "Listen, I've got to go. I love you."

"Love you, too."

I hung up and slid the phone into my pocket. Then I turned to my cousins, placed two fingers in my mouth and blew a whistle loud enough for the neighbors to hear.

"Stop it. Y'all just stop it," I fumed.

Cordelia shot Amelia a venomous look. "Garrick is coming over in less than an hour for a date and look at this mess. I can't have him seeing this. We look like an episode of *Hoarders*."

I grimaced. We sort of did.

"I'm trying to get it cleaned up," Amelia argued. "But it's taking time."

"Then hurry," Cordelia snapped.

Amelia's gaze slid to me. "If Pepper had kept that cleaning spirit spell from Snow, this wouldn't be a problem."

I raised my hands in protest. "Don't drag me into this. Besides, just because your moms conjured up a spirit easily, that doesn't mean we can, too."

"Wait." Cordelia swung her long blonde hair over one shoulder. "Our moms?"

Amelia explained what had happened.

"But I gave the slip of paper back," I explained.

"So what's this hanging out of your pocket?" Cordelia plucked something from my clothes and inspected it. A slow, devilish smile spread across her face. "It looks like a conjuring spell for a cleaning spirit."

I snatched it from her hand and had a look for myself. "How did that get in there?"

"Snow must've snuck it back in," Amelia said. "It's a sign!" She clapped her hands happily. "It's a sign that we're supposed to do the conjuring spell, call the spirit and have it help us clean these mason jars."

I gave her a pointed look. "I don't think that's what it means."

"Well, if y'all aren't going to do it, I am." Cordelia yanked the slip of paper from my fingers. As quickly as she did that, her expression filled with an apology. "Sorry, I hope you don't mind."

I nibbled my lip in worry. "I don't mind. I just don't know about this."

Amelia waved away my concern. "You saw how easy it was. Mom and Aunt Mint stood up there, chanted a few words and *voila!* They had a spirit. Then they just told it to go home. Easy peasy lemon squeezy."

My stomach twisted. "Okay. Whatever y'all say, but I have a weird feeling about this."

Cordelia patted my shoulder. "It'll be fine. Don't worry." She read the slip. "Okay, we need a few ingredients first. Amelia, grab a cauldron, batwing powder, frog's breath and cat's meow."

Amelia rushed to the hearth where Betty kept some of her ingredients as well as an extra cauldron.

"Got it all."

Cordelia took the cauldron and placed it over the everlasting fire. She filled the bowl with water, making it appear out of nowhere, and started tossing in ingredients.

"Okay, everything should turn the water green."

The three of us peered over the cauldron. The smell of decay wafted up my nose. "I don't remember it smelling like this," I murmured.

"Me neither," Amelia said, wide-eyed.

"I'm just doing what the recipe says," Cordelia said, shaking her head in annoyance. "If one of y'all would rather do it, you're welcome to it."

I folded my arms and watched the chugging, gurgling potion. "I wasn't sure about doing this in the first place."

Cordelia rolled her eyes. "Now all we have to do is say a few words." She showed each of us the paper.

Sprite of blight, sprite of spite, fill the world with your might. Chained double back and be the twixt, the one who controls you is the mistress.

Wait. Those weren't the right words.

"Stop—"

But Cordelia was already reciting. *"Sprite of blight, sprite of spite—"*

"Those aren't the right words, Cord," I said.

"Something's wrong," Amelia said.

But Cordelia didn't stop. She ignored us until the words were out of her lips and into the world.

My eyes widened as I looked at Amelia. Amelia backed away from the cauldron. "I don't think those were the words our moms said."

Cordelia flicked the paper toward us. "But y'all said it was a cleaning spell."

"Not those words." I snatched the paper from her. "These weren't them."

Cordelia's face filled with fear. "Then what did I just do?"

Amelia shook her head. "I don't know, but we'd better stand back. It looks like the cauldron's about to blow."

I'd been so focused on Cordelia that I hadn't noticed the cauldron had started to rock and sway.

"Oh no," I said. "Is there a way to stop it?"

Cordelia shouted above the trembling cauldron. "Look at the paper."

I quickly scanned it, but there was nothing else after the incantation. But I remembered what Snow had said. I snapped my fingers. "All we have to do is tell the spirit to go away. That's all. It's what Snow told me."

Amelia shrank back. "Then you'd better start telling it, because here it comes."

Yellow froth spilled from the lip of the cauldron, splashing onto the everlasting fire. The fire spat and hissed. Oh, the heart stone would probably kill me for this. I hadn't spoken to it in forever, but boy did that object have an opinion about things.

As the fire continued to protest the golden froth leaking on it, a dark figure emerged from the mouth of the cauldron.

It was an inky outline, reminding me of a shadow. It possessed a human form with a head, shoulders and torso.

But no face. The thing had absolutely no face.

"Um," Amelia's said, her voice small and quaking, "will you clean these mason jars?"

The thing launched itself toward Amelia, stopping inches from her face. Then it hissed.

"Ah," she shrieked.

"Get back," Cordelia commanded. "Go back to where you came from. If you're not going to clean and mind us, you can leave!"

The figure turned toward my cousin. "Go back," she demanded.

The inky creature floated toward Cordelia, took one…I suppose, *look* at her—that's the only way I can describe it—and then zipped straight toward the door, disappearing from the cottage.

The fire stopped hissing. The cottage quieted as the three of us stared at each other.

"What is that thing?" Cordelia said.

Amelia slowly shook her head. "I don't know, but it sure as heck didn't mind the way it was supposed to."

I fisted my hands and brought them to my chest. "That Snow. She's the one who did this. She set us up. Oh gosh, why did we have to chant that stupid spell?"

"It wasn't us." Amelia pointed to Cordelia. "It was you."

Cordelia's jaw dropped. "You're the one who told me about it. Besides"—she thrust her hand toward the jars—"we're buried under a mountain of jars."

"It's my job," Amelia shot back.

"You're pretty lousy at it. You can't even get them cleaned up."

"Stop it," I shouted. My cousins shut up and turned to me. "Blame isn't going to help us. We've got to figure this out. First off, whatever it is, it's not here to help us. The incantation was dark, using words like 'blight.'"

Amelia folded her arms. "So what are we supposed to do about it?"

"For one, we can visit Snow and find out exactly what we're dealing with."

Amelia grabbed her purse. "Great. Let's go."

"Wait." I pulled out my phone and pushed Axel's name. "First we need reinforcements."

FOUR

"*T*hanks for helping me."

Axel winked at me. "I do whatever I can to spend more time with you. Besides, I don't think there's anything to worry about yet."

"It hissed at us."

Axel was silent for a moment. "A lot of things hiss."

I grinned. "Have I ever told you how much I love your optimism?"

He wrapped a hand over my shoulder. "Have I told you I love you?"

I considered his question. Finally I answered. "I don't think so."

"Well then," he murmured in my hair. "I love you to infinity."

"Love you to infinity plus one."

"Ah!" He leaned away and pretended to have been shot in the heart. "You're killing me." His lashes lifted. Our eyes locked. A swoosh of air flooded from my lungs as Axel took my hand and kissed the back of it.

"Now," he said. "Let's find out what that thing was. Were there any clues? Anything you can remember that will help?"

Axel started up the Land Rover, and we rumbled through town on our way back to the Cobweb Forest and Snow's house.

I cringed. Of course my fiancé would ask, like, the most logical question. "It was black. Oh, and it didn't obey us when we told it to go away. Like if we conjured it, shouldn't it have listened to us?"

"Should have," he murmured.

"Amelia and Cordelia are searching for it, too, but since Snow gave me the spell, albeit without my knowledge, I figured we should go there."

Axel's right hand tightened on the steering wheel. Corded muscles popped in his forearm. Wow. Even his smallest movement was crazy sexy. "It hissed, huh?"

I nodded, dragging my gaze from his arm before I drooled onto my lap. "It hissed and disappeared out the door."

Axel was silent.

"What is it?"

"I'm not sure, but be prepared." His blue eyes snagged on mine. "It might not be good."

My heart fluttered up into my throat. "Please don't say that. We've got to stop it."

"That's what we're doing."

We entered the Cobweb Forest. The road that led into the heart of the woods was gravel and dirt. Rocks slung from the tires, bouncing off the underbelly of the truck. It sounded like we were being pelted with stones.

I curled my fingers into the seat and did my best not to seethe. "Snow Wigley better have a good reason for giving me such a horrible spell."

"Let's hope so."

It took about ten minutes for the truck to climb the winding mountain road that led to the bluff. When the blue cottage came into view, my hair stood on end.

The front door hung from its hinges. Wind slammed into the house, picking up the door and slapping it against the siding.

"What in the world?" I said.

The Land Rover ground to a halt, and Axel pulled the emergency brake. "Stay here."

I was already unbuckling my seat belt. "Like heck I will."

"Why do I even bother to request it?" Axel mused.

I curled my fingers around the door handle and opened it. "No idea."

I came around the nose of the vehicle and stood behind Axel. "Let's go slow. Be careful."

When we reached the porch, a voice sounded out from the crawl space. "Let me out!"

I glanced down to see the little possum's pink nose peeking out from the latticework.

"Hey, let me out! It might be horrible inside. Don't go in there!"

Axel's gaze darted to the possum. He placed a finger over his lips, and the possum went silent.

As quietly as possible we climbed the stairs. As if the door weighed nothing more than a slip of paper, Axel shoved it away.

Darkness lay inside. Axel motioned for me to stay behind him. I rolled my eyes and stepped through the threshold.

"Ms. Wigley? Are you here?"

Axel shot me a dark look. I smiled brightly in response.

"I'm trying to keep you safe," he said.

I shrugged. "Good luck."

"Pepper," he growled.

I patted his shoulder. "With the grace of God I defeated Lacy, who was the head of the Head Witch Order. Very little scares me now, Axel. I'm not going to be intimidated by a house with its door hanging off, whether you want to stand back or not."

"I understand, but I put your safety first."

I cocked my head and smiled. "What if she's hurt? We need to stop talking and start acting."

I wasn't trying to be difficult, but everything I had said was true. I didn't need him trying to protect me. I was a big girl, and I had proved I could take care of myself.

Rubble crunched beneath my feet. I leaned down and plucked a shattered picture frame from the floor. I scanned the rest of the room.

The house was wrecked. "Ms. Wigley?"

Axel brushed past. He'd probably decided that since I wasn't going to stay back, he should at least have a head start on me.

"Ms. Wigley," he called as he righted tables and chairs. He turned back and shot me a grim look.

I grimaced. "I know," I whispered. "It doesn't look good."

We slowly threaded our way through the house until we came to the kitchen. Axel took a step inside, stopped and ground his teeth.

"You don't want to come in here."

"What is it? Is it her?"

He nodded.

"Then I want to see."

He slowly nodded, and I followed him in. Snow Wigley sat in a chair, her mouth gaping open and her hands dangling at her sides. Her eyes had a strange hazy sheen to them, as if they were covered in cataracts. They weren't the same eyes that I'd met earlier in the day.

Her fingers were curled like claws. I noticed a slip of paper on the floor. It looked exactly like the one she had first given to me. I picked it up.

It was the correct spell, the one for the cleaning spirit. What did that mean? Had she switched the spells on purpose?

"This is the spell I was supposed to use," I said.

"But not the one you did." Axel raked his fingers through his hair. "This is bad."

I stared at her. "What happened? Was it a stroke? Heart attack?"

Axel pressed a hand to the old woman's forehead and slid it down her face, shutting her eyes. He slowly shook his head.

Axel gestured to Snow. "Heart attacks and strokes don't do that to your eyes."

"What does?"

His gaze slowly dragged around the room. He motioned for us to leave. "I don't want to talk about it in here."

I frowned. "Why not?"

"In case it's still lingering."

"What is?"

Axel cupped my elbow and guided me through the house toward his vehicle.

"It was a magic eater, wasn't it?" the possum shouted. "You can tell me. I saw part of it but wasn't sure."

Axel whirled on the creature. "How do you know that?"

The words formed dumbly on my mouth. "Magic eater?"

Axel shot the possum a scorching look. "Yes. But I wasn't going to tell you until we were safely inside the truck." He pinned an angry gaze on the possum. "In case it thought we were calling it."

"Guess I messed up your plan, huh?" the possum squealed.

Axel ignored the creature and focused on me. "Are you all right?"

Thoughts tornadoed in my mind. "Did *we* call it? Is that what we unleashed?" Bile crept up my throat. "I feel sick."

Axel rubbed my back. When our gazes met, his eyes were so full of disappointment I thought I'd throw up. "As much as I hate to say it, yes, I'm afraid you and your cousins called a magic eater into Magnolia Cove."

My lower lip trembled. I bit down on it until pain bloomed on my mouth. "What does that mean, exactly?"

"Magic eaters are difficult to deal with." Axel stared off into the distance. "Once they get started, they usually don't stop stealing magic from people until an entire town is gone, dead."

I raked my hands over my face. "So Snow is just the beginning? This—creature, will stay in Magnolia Cove until it steals the magic from every single person?"

Axel nodded sadly.

"Then what are we waiting for?" I hiked my purse onto my shoulder. "We need to get back to town and tell everyone so we can find a way to stop it."

FIVE

*A*s we headed back to the truck, the possum kept jabbering. "She's dead, isn't she? You can tell me. I have to know. I'm stuck here, you see. Stuck here under this porch, just sitting, biding my time until whatever that thing was comes back and kills me, too."

I grabbed Axel's arm and turned to him. "We can't just leave the little fellow."

"Who're you calling little fellow? I'm a girl."

"Oh I'm sorry; the deep voice made me think you were male." I was mortified. It was like asking a rather large woman when her baby was due and finding out she wasn't pregnant. I felt absolutely terrible assuming that because the possum sounded male, it was a male instead of a female.

Axel stepped to the side. "I'm going to call Garrick, get him out here while you deal with the possum." He considered a moment and leaned back into me. "Do me a favor and find out why the possum can't come out, will you?"

"I think it's spelled under there."

Something dark flashed in Axel's eyes. "Yes, but why?"

I nodded in understanding and watched as he drifted away. Time to find out if the possum would be more trouble than she was worth or if we needed her.

Of course, I also didn't want the creature to starve now that Snow was gone. Besides, it was possible the spell Snow had cast to contain it had vanished with Snow's death.

I knelt and came eye to eye with the creature. "Why are you under there?"

"Snow trapped me."

"Why?"

"Because she doesn't like possums."

A sly smile tugged the corners of my lips. "You're not a regular possum. You can talk."

"She still didn't like me."

I cocked my head at the creature. In reply the possum pawed her whiskers. "Why don't you tell me *why* Snow didn't like you?"

"She had a prejudice against rodents."

This little gal thought I was dumb. It was obvious. She figured I'd see a cute little possum trapped under a porch and be all like, let's protect animals against evil witches. But I'd been around plenty of talking creatures to know that things weren't always the way they seemed.

I started to back away. "If you don't want to tell me, that's fine. You can just stay right where you are."

"Stop," the rodent called. "Don't leave me here. What if the creature comes back?"

"Why would the creature come back?"

The possum shrugged. "I don't know. I don't speak Magic Eater. Do you?"

"How'd you know it was a magic eater?"

The possum slowly nodded. "I've seen one before."

The tops of my ears tingled with interest. "Where was that?"

The possum tugged on the lattice that now seemed like cell bars. "Let me out and I'll tell you everything. But you have to let me out."

"Stay here."

AMY BOYLES

I crossed to Axel, who'd just hung up with Garrick. "The police are on their way. I told them we'd wait."

I rubbed my shoulders. "Instead of going into town and warning everyone?"

His jaw flexed. "You go ahead."

I cringed. "I don't want to leave you alone."

He squeezed my shoulder. "I'll be fine. Besides, I'm not alone. I have a possum."

"About that." I glanced over my shoulder at the rodent, who currently gnawed on the lattice. "The possum wants out, and in exchange she'll tell us what she knows."

Axel stared in the creature's direction. "Do you think she has information?"

"Hard to say."

A breeze ticked up and slid through Axel's hair. He grimaced. "There's no time to play it safe right now, not when people might be in danger. I say we let her out."

I nodded. "I'll follow your lead."

The possum had disappeared back into the cavernous depths of the crawl space. Axel strode over to the lattice, and in one quick movement he ripped a patch of the white crisscrossed wood away.

"Easy enough," he murmured.

"Are you in there?" I called.

Suddenly the little critter darted through the hole. She stood on her hind legs and reached for the sky.

"Years of not being able to stretch will give you such a tight spine. Oh, this feels good. It feels so wonderful to stand to my full height! Anyway, thanks for all your help. I appreciate it. Now I'll just be going."

Before the possum could scamper away, Axel grabbed her by the scruff of the neck. "Hold on a minute. You got a name?"

"Flower."

"Flower the Possum," Axel said, straight-faced. I nearly laughed at such a sweet name on such a prickly furred creature, but I let it go.

Axel studied the possum. "Flower, you suggested to Pepper that

30

you knew something. Let me tell you what I know—my fiancée and her cousins summoned the creature accidentally. It came from a spell that Snow had given them. But why would Snow have them summon a creature that would only return and claim her?"

The possum pawed the air, clearing wanting down. "Maybe Snow had a death wish? Maybe she handed them the wrong spell?"

I placed the slip of paper with the correct spell in front of the possum. "This was the right spell. Somehow I ended up with the wrong one. It was switched."

Flower blinked at the paper. "Oh no, then someone changed it. One of the people at the meeting must have done it."

"But who?" I said.

"Ask your grandmother. Betty Craple would know."

I reached out and took Flower away from Axel. "Perfect, let's go, Possum. You can help me."

"No." The rodent struggled in my arms. "I'm free now. I've told you everything I know."

"Rodent," Axel growled.

The possum's fur bristled.

Fury flashed in Axel's eyes. "You give Pepper a hard time, and I'll stuff you back under that house and curse you there for all eternity."

"Okay," Flower whimpered. "I'll help."

Axel's shoulders relaxed. "Good. Pepper, get back to the house. Do you want to take the truck?"

I shook my head. "Can you transport us there?"

Axel nodded. "Hold still."

I clasped Flower to my chest, and in one swift motion the house slipped away and we were heading back to Betty's in Magnolia Cove.

"WE HAVE a magic eater on the loose."

I was back at home with Flower tucked under one arm. Amelia and Cordelia had found Betty, and we stood in the living room in front of the hearth fire.

"Snow is dead. Axel said her body looked like the work of a magic eater, and Flower here confirmed it."

Betty stared at the three of us. A wind blew from an unseen vortex and whipped Betty's wig off. My eyelids widened. A lightning bolt struck out, causing the house to tremble.

When Betty spoke, I swear another being had taken over her body. Her eyes turned liquid black, and pure anger wafted off my grandmother in sheets.

The wind slapped my hair against my face. My clothes ruffled against the force.

Betty's mouth opened. "Why the heck did y'all release a magic eater?"

"We were tricked," I yelled above the wind. "Snow slipped a spell into my pocket. It was supposed to be the same spell that Mint and Licky used, but when Cordelia read it, it wasn't."

Betty took a menacing step toward us. My cousins and I huddled together as the wind started knocking objects over. A bud vase toppled to the floor, and books cascaded from shelves.

"I told you I didn't like Snow. Isn't that enough not to trust her?"

My face stung as hair whipped my cheeks. "Betty, stop it! Snow is dead. Someone else slipped me the wrong spell, counting on the fact that I would perform the incantation. The magic eater feasted on her. So as strange as it may seem," I yelled, "Snow is innocent in all this. I'm pretty certain."

Ever so slowly the breeze faded. After a moment Betty picked up her wig and slid it on, back side facing front.

"Um…" Cordelia shyly pointed toward it. "Your wig is…um…"

Betty wagged her finger at my cousin. "I don't want to hear one word out of you. Not one word. You're the cause of all this."

"Betty," I said gently, "the magic eater may be after more people. Since it targeted Snow, I don't know if there are other targets or if the creature will work at random. But Axel suggested it would feast on our town. No matter what, it needs to be contained and quickly. My first question is, why would a magic eater go after Snow?"

Betty exhaled a deep breath and slumped into a chair. "There were six of them."

I shot my cousins a questioning glance. Cordelia and Amelia shrugged. They didn't know this story any more than I did.

Time to listen up.

"Three witches and three wizards. Snow was one. Twenty years ago they summoned a great evil—something dark, inky black."

As she spoke, Betty's eyes became glassy. Whatever she was seeing in her mind, it was far, far away.

"They thought it was controllable, but the witches and wizards quickly realized they couldn't contain the evil they had brought into Magnolia Cove."

"Was it another magic eater?" Cordelia said.

Betty shook her head. "Worse. It was a blight on the town. It caused the crops to die, the water to go bad. The magic they unleashed was pure evil. Since six had worked together to harness it, those same six were the ones who had to send it back to the depths of hell."

A shiver ran up my spine. This was definitely not bedtime-story material. "Where did they send it?"

Betty shook her head, that vacant look still on her face. "I don't know, but they ended its curse on the town. If the blight ever returned to Magnolia Cove, they would have to be the ones to stop it."

She rubbed her chin, stopping to finger a hair. She pinched it between two fingers and ripped it from its socket. "And now one of them is dead." Betty inhaled sharply and shuddered. "That means that either one of the other five called the magic eater, or everyone who is left is on the list, too. Either way, that's where we start."

I placed Flower on the couch. "Okay. Who are they and where do we start?"

"The first is Sylvia Spirits."

My jaw dropped. Sylvia Spirits was an upstanding citizen of Magnolia Cove.

"But Sylvia always helped you with the spell that kept Rufus out," I argued, "when he wasn't allowed into town. She's not bad."

"She was misguided in her youth," Betty said.

"The second is Charlie James Hix."

As if it wasn't possible for my jaw to drop any farther, it did. "CJ Hix? The real estate agent? The guy who says 'golly gee' and calls me Miss Dunn? Him?" I fisted a hand to my hip in protest. "Isn't CJ too young to have helped Snow twenty years ago? What is he, like, thirty?"

My grandmother shook her head. "He was very young when Snow snagged him. Her cousin. Saw the potential. Yes, he was still a child when they summoned the blight. But that was twenty years ago, and there's no telling what CJ has really grown up into."

I scowled. "I don't see CJ as the sort of person to call a magic eater."

Betty waved my protest away with a flick of her hand. "Let me finish. The next wizard was Saltz Swift."

Now that I could buy. The headmaster of the Southern School of Magic was someone who generally made the hair on the back of my neck stand on end.

"And they let him run a school?" Amelia said, surprised. "Are they kidding?"

"Like I said, these witches and wizards have been on the straight and narrow for years. They've proven themselves solid members of society. I forgave them. Not Snow, but the others."

Cordelia tapped her foot. "And the last two?"

"Forbes Henry," Betty said mysteriously, "one of the richest men in Magnolia Cove and a hermit."

"He's not a hermit anymore. He was at the meeting today," I murmured.

"And the last witch that joined the group—" She stared at us, her gaze dragging from me to my cousins.

I held my breath, waiting to hear who was the final witch to have caused a great evil to land on Magnolia Cove, but Betty hedged.

"Who was it?" Amelia said.

Betty cleared her throat. "It was me."

SIX

"*I* told you to ask Betty," Flower said.

"Who are you?" Betty directed to the possum, but shrieks coming from Amelia stole our attention.

"Are you kidding? You always, and I mean *always,* get onto us for doing stuff wrong, and you brought a blight on the town? Oh, this is rich."

Amelia folded her arms and raised her nose. "I'm never listening to you again."

Betty shot from her chair so fast I wasn't sure she'd ever been sitting it. Her bosom hit Amelia right in the stomach and nearly knocked my cousin over.

"Hey," Amelia shouted.

Betty glowered. "Let me tell you something, kid. It's because of my mistakes that I can tell y'all what to do, and that's precisely why you *should* listen to me."

Amelia whimpered. "You always win."

"Because I'm old and ornery. Snow tricked us. She said what we were summoning wasn't anything evil, but it was. Now there's a magic eater—and it might be coming for me."

That sobered us up and quieted us down. Betty pinned her attention back on Flower. "How'd you wind up with Snow?"

"She caught me out in the woods and stuck me under the crawl space, angry at me for eating from her garden. I've only now just gotten free." The possum spoke quickly, her words tumbling over one another like a babbling brook. "I could hear what Snow said from the house, and she said your name a lot."

Flower's gaze flickered to mine. "That's how I knew you should ask your grandmother."

"How'd you know to recognize a magic eater?" I said.

Flower shrugged. "Because I'd seen one once before. Snow had summoned it. I don't know why—not this one, but another one. She spoke to it and then banished it."

Betty rubbed her chin. "So Snow was up to her old tricks. No surprise there. But how can you speak to us?"

The possum shook her head. "Snow cursed me. Made it so I could speak and understand language and then locked me in the crawl space."

"Oh, you poor little guy," Amelia said. "I'm so sorry."

"I'm not a guy," Flower said. "I'm a girl, but Snow gave me a male voice."

Amelia shot Betty a hopeful look. "Maybe we can help Flower sound like a female."

Betty grabbed her handbag and hooked it on her arm. "First things first—we've got to warn the others. Assuming one of the six is the person who sent the magic eater after us, then they must be told."

"But why would one of them do this?" I mused. "Why now? After all this time?"

Betty tugged her wig. "Why, I've got this on backward." After righting the hairpiece, she glanced at me. "I don't know. Maybe one of them wants revenge. Maybe they're mad at us for all being a part of it. If I had to guess who was to blame, I'd say Forbes. He was always so smarmy. Thinking he was in charge and could tell us all what to do. Well, maybe this is his last laugh. He's an old man. Who knows? But I do know we need to question them—all of them, right now."

She had just turned the knob when a scream sliced through the quiet.

"That sounded like Sylvia." Betty slung the door open. "Come on, girls! Let's help my friend!"

~

WE RACED down the street until we reached Charming Conical Caps. Betty barged inside and found Sylvia curled up on a divan. Her red hair swam around her face. Her eyes were wide and shining, and she trembled from head to foot.

Betty fisted her hands to her hips. "Let me guess-it's been here."

Sylvia's red lips moved, but no words came out. She flung herself at Betty, nearly falling to the floor before my grandmother took hold of the much taller woman.

"I never thought that in my entire life I'd see such a creature," Sylvia cried. "It came for me. If I hadn't been paying attention, I never would've been able to stop it."

She pulled away and glanced at her shaking hands. "I don't know how I fought it off and won. Next time I may not be so lucky."

"Let's hope there isn't a next time," Betty murmured. "Sylvia, I hate to tell you this, but one of the six called the magic eater here. Snow is dead."

Tears poured down Sylvia's eyes. "No! It can't be."

"It is." Betty clasped her hands. "We have to tell the others and form a meeting."

Sylvia inhaled sharply. She smoothed her dress, dragged her fingers under her lashes to fix any makeup smudges and clapped her hands.

The scores of hats pegged around the room melted away, and I found myself in a room with black walls.

"Whoa, that was cool," I said.

"And I thought Snow had power," Flower said. "That was amazing."

Six mirrors hung on the walls. They were about the same size—three feet long and two feet across, and each was framed in gold but the design was different. The first was a basic square frame, nothing ornate. They seemed to become more ornate as the frames continued, with the last one having lots of curling scrollwork.

"Snow is dead," Sylvia announced.

A black drape appeared and covered the farthest mirror. Light flared within the other mirrors like they were illuminating from the inside out.

"Cool," Amelia whispered.

Cordelia shot her a dark look, and Amelia replied with her own scowl.

"Don't look at me like that. You're the entire reason we're in this mess. All because you couldn't let Garrick see a little mess. Now Garrick's got a murder to deal with."

Cordelia's eyes narrowed to slits, but she said nothing.

"Trouble in paradise," Flower whispered.

If the possum had been a person, I would've elbowed her in the ribs. But as it was, she was a slightly smelly possum tucked under my arm.

"We call the three," Sylvia and Betty said in unison. "Call the three to meet."

The mirrors glowed, and suddenly three faces appeared in front of us. CJ Hix's blue eyes were troubled.

Saltz Swift appeared in another mirror. The headmaster's dark hair was slicked back with oil, and a deep frown was set in his mouth.

The last mirror filled with the man I'd seen at the meeting—Forbes Henry. Forbes Henry had salt-and-pepper hair with a trimmed mustache. His face was gaunt, and the hollows of his cheeks looked like someone had scooped them clear with an ice cream dipper.

"What's the meaning of this meeting?" Forbes said angrily. "Why've you called us here?"

"Yes," Saltz said tersely. "I have a night class to teach, so this had better be important."

"Someone has murdered Snow," Betty said. "They've set a magic eater on the loose. It just attacked Sylvia, but she was able to thwart it."

CJ frowned. "Golly, why would someone do that?"

Betty pointed at the men in the mirror. "We were all at the meeting today. Someone slipped my granddaughter an incantation to call the creature. Which one of you was it?"

Forbes scoffed. "You think I would want to kill the old bat after all these years? If I'd wanted her dead, I would have done so ages ago."

Saltz sniffed. "The same. What we did is in the past. Perhaps Snow called the creature herself as a final way to get back at all of us."

"Is it coming after us?" CJ said, his voice fluttering with panic.

"I believe so," Betty said grimly. "We need to find a way to send it back."

Forbes scowled. Deep lines etched into both sides of his mouth. "If Snow called it and she's dead, there's no way of getting rid of it until the magic eater has done its job."

"They might have had a contract," Saltz said. "A contract that bound the magic eater to do Snow's bidding. If that's the case, then Forbes is right."

"We have to try." Sylvia pounded a fist into her hand. "We must find a way to contain it. What if it starts feeding on the rest of the town?"

"That's gonna be bad," CJ said.

Seriously. I couldn't believe that somehow golden boy CJ Hix had ended up working with much older witches and wizards to call down a blight on the town. He simply seemed way too goofy and nice to do anything so terrible.

"We have to stop it," Betty said.

Saltz gazed around the room. "I see your granddaughter, Pepper. Send her to the school to go through the spell books. There may be a way to cease a magic eater from completing its contract."

Betty nodded. "What else?"

"Y'all are full of phooey." Forbes swatted the air. "If someone else dies, call me. Otherwise, I'm staying out of this."

"You're making a mistake," Sylvia said.

"I don't think so," Forbes griped.

With that, he vanished and his mirror went dark.

"I'll help however I can," CJ said.

"You work with the police," Betty commanded. "You may be able to help out some way. Keep your defenses up. You'll need them."

CJ peered out to me and my cousins. "Good to see you, Miss Dunn."

I waved. "You too, CJ."

Betty shot me an incredulous look, and I dropped my hand. CJ disappeared, leaving Saltz Swift.

"Miss Dunn, I'll expect you at the school."

"Yes, sir," I said before Saltz disappeared.

Betty gazed at us. "Cordelia and Amelia, I want you to help the police however you can. Tell them the spell you used to call the creature." Her gaze darted to me. "And you're going to the school. Take the possum with you. Saltz may be able to use her knowledge to help figure out a good counter spell."

My grandmother sighed. Her shoulder's sagged, and for a moment she looked defeated. I clasped a hand on her shoulder. "It's going to be okay. We can fight this."

Betty looked up at me. Her eyes were filled with sadness. "I hope so. This is a bad situation we're in. Let's see if we can get out of it."

I dropped my hand, and Sylvia coiled her arm around Betty. "We will all fight this together. As best we can."

"But we first have to figure out who called it. Was it one of them?" Betty scratched her chin. "Did Forbes do it?"

"He barely spoke," I said.

"I'd say he's suspicious," Amelia seconded.

"He didn't act like he cared at all," Cordelia added.

Betty pulled her corncob pipe from a pocket and slid it between her teeth. She lit the bowl and sucked hard on the tobacco.

"Looks like we'll have to pay Forbes a visit." Betty exhaled and a perfect smoke ring flittered to the ceiling. "But first, y'all have your assignments. We've got to figure out a way to at least slow the creature down, if not stop it."

I shouldered my purse and tightened my hold on Flower. "Leave it to us. We'll help figure out a way to stop this magic eater. It's not going to kill anyone else—not on my watch."

SEVEN

The streets of Magnolia Cove were quiet as we walked back.

"News has spread," Betty said quietly. "The people know and they're in their homes, hoping that the magic eater doesn't come for them."

I grimaced. The weight of this pushed down on my shoulders. But all I could do was work to right the situation.

"Betty, you can't be alone," I said. "Not with that creature out lurking."

"We plan on keeping her within our sight." Amelia hugged Betty. I guess she'd gotten over her initial irritation at my grandmother about her past. "We won't let anything happen to you."

Betty jutted out her chin. "Let's not focus on that. Let's focus on doing what we can." She turned to me. "Pepper, I'll magic you to the school. If I see Axel, I'll send him your way as well."

I nodded in thanks.

"You ready?"

I glanced down at Flower. "*You* ready?"

The possum tucked her furry face into my arm. "As ready as I'll ever be."

The last thing I needed for Betty to see was my worry, so I plastered on a big smile. "I'm ready."

Betty pressed a finger to her nose. Sparkles of magic flitted from her nostril and whirled around me. Next thing I knew, Flower and I were standing in the foyer of the Southern School of Magic.

"Can you please put me down?" Flower said. "It's not like I'm going to run off and leave you."

I gently placed the possum on the floor. A figure sweeping down the staircase caught my attention, and I locked eyes with Saltz Swift.

The headmaster gestured in greeting. "Miss Dunn, I'm so glad to see you."

His hands slid over mine. His touch was cold. Ice shards pricked up the backs of my hands all the way to my elbows. I fought off the shiver that threatened to take over.

"Master Swift, so good to see you."

He kissed the air beside my cheek. "We really should try to meet under better circumstances than these."

I quirked a brow. "You mean not when everything's falling apart?"

"Exactly." He smiled but the warmth didn't reach his eyes. The headmaster pointed a toe at the possum. "And who is your guest?"

"This is Flower. Snow had her locked under the crawl space of her house. The possum saw the magic eater and may be able to help."

Swift gave a curt nod. "Follow me to the library."

Within minutes Flower and I were standing in a chamber lined with books. The ceilings were twelve feet high, and every single inch was covered in leather-bound tomes. The air smelled of dried paper and animal hide. I inhaled deeply as those were two of my favorite scents.

Swift gestured with a flourish. "The back wall holds the spell books that deal with magical creatures. You'll want to start there. I'll check in on you in a few hours, see how you're holding up."

I shot Flower a hopeful glance. "We'll do our best to get through as many as possible."

"I'll leave you to it." Swift turned to leave. "Oh, and Pepper?"

"Yes?"

Swift smiled; this time it wasn't as cold. "Good luck. Our lives depend on it. I would stay, but I have a class to teach."

I thanked Swift and he disappeared.

Flower scampered onto a thickly cut wooden table. "Now, which one would you like to try first?"

I scanned the titles. "How about *Magical Creatures for Beginners?*"

"Sounds like a winner." The possum darted up the wall until she reached the book, snagged it between her two front teeth and pulled until it slowly slid from the shelf.

She grabbed it with her two paws and jumped back onto the table right in front of me.

"Ta-da! Here you go."

I patted her head. "Impressive."

"You should see what I can do with a cherry stem."

I clicked my tongue. "Maybe another time." I peeled back the cover. The stale smell of previously wet paper wafted from the book. "Whew. I wonder when this one was last opened?"

"Looks like it's been a while."

I closed my eyes, said a silent prayer that we'd find something useful and started flipping through.

We'd been at it a couple of hours. I sat at the table, a pile of books surrounding me. My back and shoulders ached from hunching, and a headache bloomed in my skull.

Flower had easily retrieved twenty books for me, and we'd scanned all of them quickly, searching for information about magic eaters. But what we'd learned so far had been limited. Nothing that really helped us.

I was already getting frustrated. I raked my fingers through my hair, hoping to wake up my brain. Was I missing something? Was there something I wasn't seeing?

I couldn't let despair overtake me. I had to keep cool and calm or else I might overlook something.

"You know, for once I'd like to have a real date."

Axel's voice cut through the haze of my brain. I blinked and smiled, pivoting toward the sound.

A dark look crossed his face, but Axel quickly smiled when our gazes locked. I rose and wrapped my arms around him.

Axel gave me a solid squeeze. The warmth of his body felt like heaven. I tipped my chin up and smiled.

"We had a real date when you asked me to marry you," I remarked.

Axel's lips curled into a luscious smile. "Hopefully not our only one." He nodded toward the table. "How's this going?"

"Flower and I've been searching through old books, but it's not going well. How're things in the outside world?"

A low growl emanated from Axel's throat. "It's going. Garrick's men are on high alert. They're swarming the town, keeping watch over some of the witches who may be in danger."

"Like Betty?"

Axel nodded. He threaded his fingers through his hair and slumped to a chair. "What a mess."

"I agree," Flower said stoutly. "We've picked through a lot of information, but there's very little that helps."

Axel rubbed his chin and stared at the wall. "What have you learned so far?"

I stumbled over my words. "Not much. Magic eaters are spirits that feed on the power of others, generally sucking a person dry of their magic and, in the process, killing them."

Axel squinted at the books. "Yes, we know that. We also know the spirit was summoned." He snapped his fingers and rose. Axel crossed to the left of the bookcase, walking down to the far edge.

"Saltz Swift said the books we wanted are over here," I protested.

"But what if they're not?" Axel reached up and pulled down a book that didn't look nearly as old as the others. "Aha!"

"What's that?" I said.

"This might help us. At least it might give us an idea for protection."

"Yes, but what is it?"

"This is called the *Catchings and Conjurings of Creatures Mythical*. Sounds like a winner."

"Impressive," Flower said.

I froze. There was something familiar about that title. Something I couldn't place. I stared at it. The binding looked familiar, too.

Axel placed it on the table. The binding cracked as it opened. Beautiful colored images snaked across the pages. The first held an animated unicorn. The creature threw its head back into the sky and reared up, pawing the air.

The creature seemed to look at us and snort in impatience.

"Can it see us?" I said.

Axel nodded. "It's in there. Trapped on the page."

I curled my fingers into Axel's arm. "I know where I saw this book. At Snow's! She said she'd trapped these creatures. How did this book end up here if it was at her house?"

"Do you think Saltz brought it?" I said.

"Maybe," Axel replied. "Or perhaps it's a copy?"

I shook my head. "No. I don't think so. From the way Snow talked, she made it seem that she personally had trapped every single creature in this book."

Axel quirked a brow. "She would have to be very old to have trapped some of them. A few of these creatures are extinct. It might've been passed down."

"But why is it here?" I said.

Axel flipped the page to a troll. The small stout creature threw an axe over his shoulder and glared at us. "Are you going to just stand there and stare at me all day, or are you going to call me out of this book?"

My jaw dropped. "Holy cow."

"And as we see," Axel said, "this book holds many different creatures."

I touched the binding. The troll shouted obscenities at me. I flinched but ignored his harsh words. "But it's only a book."

Flower scurried over to us. "But it's very magical."

Axel nodded. "Right. There are probably three hundred entries in here. From unicorns to krakens—this book holds them all."

"And you think it might have an entry about the magic eater?"

"If we're lucky."

Oh my gosh, if that were true, that would mean Snow had the magic eater all along. Had she been the one to summon it?

Axel flipped the pages one by one. I spotted demons and Pegasus, cupids and gorgons, until we reached the rear of the book.

"This part holds the lesser known or more rare entries." Axel peeled back page after page until he shouted, "There!"

He must've found what he was looking for. I smiled with pride. He was so smart, this fiancé of mine. I was one lucky gal.

He proceeded to read. "'The magic eater, once summoned, will eat until either the beast has fulfilled an obligation or until there is no magic left for it to digest.'"

I shuddered. "That would mean the creature would devour all of us in Magnolia Cove."

"'This creature goes by the name *Erebus*, and will work tirelessly until it has completed its duty.'"

Axel stopped talking. I peered over his shoulder and stared at the page.

"Where is it?" I said, afraid of the answer.

Axel turned the book upside down. The pages converged in the center, and a world of creatures yelled and hissed at us.

"Opinionated, aren't they?" I said.

Axel didn't say anything. He flipped the book back over and shoved papers away until he reached the page once more.

Still blank.

He exhaled a low whistle. "Erebus the Magic Eater that you and your cousins summoned, came from this book. He was called from his prison in here and set loose in Magnolia Cove."

My chest tightened in excitement. The tone of Axel's voice suggested it might be easy to chain the creature back to the book.

"How difficult will it be to return him?"

Axel closed the book with a thump and tucked it under his arm. "Hopefully not too bad. Maybe we can trap him back in these pages. We just have to find him."

"And the words we have to say?" I said.

Axel tapped the cover. "I need to think about that. But what I'm concerned with is that whoever slipped you the wrong piece of paper summoned the magic eater from this book, which means they knew all about it."

My stomach seized as I realized what was really going on. "Saltz Swift was at Snow's today, and now the book is here—and he didn't tell me about it." I lowered my voice. "He told us to stick to this wall. But you found this book on another one."

Axel pursed his lips. "I don't know if Saltz is guilty, but we need to keep a close eye on him."

Axel waved a hand over the mess of tomes I had strewn over the table. One by one they lifted and returned to their spots on the wall.

He gave me a tired smile. "Come on. Let's get out of here."

I scooped up Flower and tucked her under my arm. "We need to find Saltz first," I said. "He said he was going to check on us soon, but he never showed up."

A scream split the air. I shot Axel a look, and we raced from the library back into the corridors of the school. We followed the sound of the scream to the foyer.

A crowd of people ran toward the same place, surrounding the young student who had screamed.

The girl took a step back and pointed down. Slumped on the floor, his face pale and drained of life, lay the body of the former headmaster, Saltz Swift.

EIGHT

The police had been called, and I sat outside, my hands trembling as I held the book that had contained the magic eater.

"Are you okay?" Axel said.

I closed my eyes tight and shook my head. "I feel so horrible. I liked Saltz Swift. He was a decent headmaster and was good to me. He let me teach a class. I guess now we know he didn't put the book in the library."

"My guess is it ended there possibly as part of the summoning spell." Axel wrapped an arm around my shoulder. "There may be more in the book. A protection ward. We're going to need it because the way that thing's moving, we'll have to round up your grandmother and the others who might be affected."

My eyes widened. "But how can we protect them? Saltz was a powerful wizard." Then I remembered. "Sylvia Spirits was attacked, but she managed to fight it off."

Or had she? No one had seen Sylvia with Erebus. All we had heard was her scream, and then she had claimed the creature attacked her.

I frowned. Sylvia wasn't the type of person to have had me and my cousins summon something so evil.

Was she?

I pressed the heels of my hands to my eyes. What a disaster. But I had to focus on the now. "Okay. It's starting to get late. We need to come up with a serious protection spell or figure out a way to keep Betty and the rest of them safe through the night. Then we can focus on catching the creature during the day. As a magic eater, he'll probably be more powerful at night, but if we can find him during the day, we may be at an advantage. How does that sound?"

Axel smiled at me proudly. "Sounds like a plan."

CJ, Sylvia, Betty and my cousins were all back at my house. Garrick Young, the sheriff, had arrived and informed them of what happened to Saltz Swift.

"I'll stay through the night," Garrick said, "keeping watch outside."

We all thanked him, and Garrick went to sit on the porch, to make sure nothing that wasn't supposed to enter our house would.

Axel showed Betty, CJ and Sylvia the book. "The creature was summoned from here," he explained.

"*Catchings and Conjurings of Creatures Mythical*," Betty nearly whispered. "I know this book from somewhere."

"Me too," Sylvia said, "but I can't think of where."

Axel tapped the cover. "According to Pepper, it's from Snow's house. I came across it in the library at the school."

"Strange," Betty said.

"Let's see if there's anything we can find in here that points to protection," Axel said, steering the conversation back to the present.

CJ, Betty and Sylvia poured over the pages, devouring the words that Axel and I had perused only hours earlier.

"I'm going to make some hot tea," I said. "Does anyone want some?"

A couple of people murmured yes, so I trudged off into the kitchen to make tea. I found Flower inside. She had stretched her paws onto a window and was looking out, chanting low. When she finished, the possum glanced over her shoulder and jumped.

I smiled. "You performing a protection spell?"

Flower worried her hands. "Of course. I don't want to die, and I heard Snow say them enough times."

"You heard her from under the crawl space?"

"Oh, I eventually chewed through a little bit of flooring and slipped upstairs every once in a while. I was still trapped by the boundaries of the house, but seeing new scenery helped."

"I'm sorry Snow trapped you."

Flower perched onto a chair and studied me with her dark eyes. "It's okay."

"Maybe when all this is over we can help you get back to where you came from."

"That would be wonderful," Flower mused. "To run free in the forest is all I want."

I put the kettle on and sat at the table across from her. "Tell me, what did you see before Snow died?"

The possum arched an eyebrow. "You want to know what the magic eater looked like?"

"I think I know what it looks like." I drummed my nails on the table. "What I want to know is, was there anything that warned of the intruder?"

Flower seemed to think about it for a moment as she placed a paw under her chin. "I don't remember any sort of warning. It just arrived like a tornado. You saw what a mess Snow's house was in."

I nodded. "I did."

Images of the mess crashed down on me. The weight of the two dead bodies I'd seen today made tears prick my eyes. I didn't like Snow, but I didn't want her dead—much less to be the catalyst for her demise.

Betty could be next. The idea that such a nasty creature would hurt my grandmother simply made me angry.

"Why?" I closed my eyes tight. "Why did this have to happen?"

Sympathy filled Flower's dark eyes. She dipped her head. "I'm sorry, Pepper. But maybe we can stop it."

Axel swept into the kitchen holding a dark stone that looked like obsidian. He chanted another protection spell. When he was done, my fiancé turned to me.

"This is the last room and should hold us till the morning." He slipped the stone in his pocket and stared at me.

Flower's gaze shifted from Axel to me. She seemed to sense that he wanted to speak with me privately, so she hopped up and scurried to the door.

"I'll just wait out here for my tea," the possum said.

I rose and turned the heat down so that Axel and I would have a few extra minutes alone.

"Are you watching Sylvia?" I whispered.

He nodded. "She saw it, you say?"

"Yes."

We stared at each other. Axel was thinking the same thing I was—how could Sylvia have survived when Saltz hadn't? It made no sense.

"We both watch her," Axel whispered. "If I notice anything suspicious, I'll tell you."

"And if I see her call a demon, I'll scream for you—how's that?"

Axel smiled grimly. "And just when I thought we'd have a few hours to figure out where to get married, we're sucked into a life-or-death situation."

I wanted to make a joke, but I was dry. There was nothing I could say that held any sort of amusement because none of this was funny.

"Flower said the magic eater gave no warning—except tornado-like winds." I cocked a brow. "Did you give the book to Garrick?"

Axel shook his head. "I'm afraid the creature might rip it from his hands."

I balked. "Doesn't he need protection?"

Axel rapped his knuckles on the table. "He's not the one Erebus is after."

I bit my lower lip in thought. "If you think so."

"I'll stay outside with him."

I grasped Axel's arm. "No. I don't want you in danger."

He smirked. Axel picked up my hand and tenderly kissed each finger before pressing it to his chest. "We all have to fight this thing. Even if it—God forbid—accomplishes its task, who's to say Erebus won't then attack the rest of the town?"

Axel was right. I kissed him and crossed to the stove, turning up the kettle until steam poured from the spout and the sound of its whistle filled the kitchen.

"I'll keep an eye on Sylvia. You stay with Garrick."

Axel rose. His jaw tightened. "It's a plan."

I SETTLED the rattling tea service on a table. My heart jumped into my throat, pulsing at the hollow of my neck. I had to watch Sylvia like a hawk and somehow coax her into explaining exactly how she fought off a magic eater.

My friend. A woman who had helped us plenty of times I had to get information out of. The thought made me nervous as heck.

Cordelia and Amelia played checkers by the fire. Betty rocked in her chair, humming a song to herself. A skein of yarn lay by her feet, and needles clacked as my grandmother knitted.

Betty was clearly stressed to the max. Never before had I seen her knit anything.

I didn't even know she could.

I created a teacup for each woman and nestled it beside them. When I was finished, I poured a cup for myself and sat across from Sylvia.

"Where's CJ?" I said.

"Outside with the men." Sylvia raked her red fingernails through her hair. "He'll come in after a while to get some rest."

"Isn't it dangerous for him to be out there?"

She shrugged. "I think he'd rather be with the men than the woman right now."

"I can understand that," Flower said from her spot curled up by the fireplace. "Part of me would rather be with them."

My gaze darted to the stairs. "Where's Hugo?"

"With the men," Betty said.

"Sounds about right," I murmured. I turned my attention back to Sylvia. "I'm so amazed that you survived the magic eater."

Sylvia curled her legs under and leaned back on the couch. "I really don't know how I did it. I was standing in my shop and heard a loud noise. Next thing I knew a dark mass, like a combination between a cloud and mist, drifted into the store."

Her voice quaked. "I'd never seen one before, but no one had to tell me it was pure evil. My hand shot out as if it had a will of its own, and I shouted a banishing spell. It wasn't anything specific, so I knew whatever it was would come back, but it was enough to keep the magic eater from killing me."

"It took Saltz Swift in the school," I said. "He had left Flower and me to teach a class and got caught. I'm sure he was on guard."

Sylvia nodded absently. "It wasn't enough. Honestly, I considered myself lucky to have survived. Under any other circumstances I don't think I would've made it." She dropped her head into her hands. "Poor Saltz. He wasn't always the best person, but he would never have done this. Never would've cursed us.

"It's just so horrible." Tears dripped down Sylvia's face, and in that moment I didn't think she was guilty of having summoned the magic eater. But if she didn't, who did?

Forbes Henry, that's who I figured.

"Does Forbes know y'all were camping out here tonight?" I said.

Betty nodded. "The stubborn old coot didn't want to come. Said he'd take his chances. If he's still alive tomorrow, I say we hang him upside down and pinch a clothespin over his nose until he confesses."

"I agree," Amelia said. "If he can outlive Saltz and Snow, he must be behind all this."

I agreed. We women in the room all stared at one another, silently contemplating how we would torture an old man into confessing.

How warped I was. I cringed at my thoughts. But at least I knew I wasn't the only one having them.

The wind howled outside and I shivered. I hoped the men would be okay. I worried that even with the protection spell on the house, it wouldn't be enough.

A screech came from outside. The five of us bolted from our seats. I raced to the door.

"Don't go out there," Betty snapped. "The protection spell only works with the door shut. If the magic eater is out there and you open the door, you risk letting it inside."

"But we have the book," I said.

Betty and Sylvia shifted into uncomfortable silence. That's when I realized the worst of the worst.

"Y'all are scared, aren't you?"

Neither woman answered.

From outside the men yelled. I whirled on Betty and Sylvia. "In all the time I've been in Magnolia Cove, the two of y'all have never been afraid of anything. Now you're scared? Well, what if this magic eater wants more than just you six? What if it wants the entire town?"

I fisted my hands as I stared into their guilt-ridden faces. "Are y'all just gonna sit here while those men fight for you?"

No one moved. I darted to the book and grasped it between both hands.

I ran toward the door, and in a flash of magic, Betty was standing in front of it, blocking my path.

"Pepper, you must wait!"

"Why?"

"See if the men can stop it first," she said.

"Why? I don't understand."

Betty's lower lip trembled. "There's a clause in the magic eater's spell."

The men shouted. The wind howled. It sounded like a tree had been ripped from its roots.

"What are you talking about, a clause?"

Betty's gaze shifted to Sylvia. Sylvia elbowed Betty. "Tell her."

"You'd better tell her," Cordelia said. "My boyfriend is out there."

"So's my fiancé," I said. "If you're going to be sitting in here like chickens while they're outside fighting, you'd better tell us all about this clause.'"

Betty worried her hands. "It's in the book—under an asterisk at the very bottom of Erebus's page. You need a magnifying glass to see it. If you don't get Erebus back into the book willingly, he'll wreak even further havoc."

"That's ridiculous," I said. "Tricking him is getting him in there unwillingly."

Betty frowned. "It's dangerous."

I couldn't leave Axel and the other men out there any longer.

"I'll take the risk." I opened the front door, fully prepared to be flinging a book at a scary magic eater, but instead found myself head-smacking into someone.

"Ouch," I yelled. "What the heck?"

"Get out of my way." A body stormed past me. I glanced up, shocked to see the salt-and-pepper-covered head of Forbes Henry standing in the doorway.

He brushed off his shoulders. "I'm seeking shelter."

Lightning cracked outside, illuminating the doorframe. Forbes Henry's tall but brittle body glowed in the light. He was old—at least eighty—with a very serious frown. He moved slowly with the help of a golden-eagle-topped cane.

He stared at us. "Well? Isn't anyone going to offer me something to drink? I had to outrun a magic eater to get here and nearly died trying."

We all looked at one another. I glanced at the teapot. "Let me fix you something."

Forbes yanked a fedora off his head and tossed it on the couch. "Put a shot of bourbon in it. That'll help my nerves so I can tell y'all the story."

My gaze flickered to Axel, who stood behind Forbes. Axel nodded to me. He smirked in disbelief. "Let's get you comfortable, Mr. Henry, so you can tell us exactly how you managed to outrun a magic eater."

NINE

*F*orbes Henry sat on the couch while we gathered around.

Axel kept shooting me glances that suggested he didn't trust Forbes one bit.

I don't think anyone did.

The two of us stood by the far wall, our heads together while Forbes, with shaking hands, sucked down his hot tea and bourbon.

"I spoke to Sylvia," I whispered into Axel's ear.

His head turned slightly toward me, and I got a whiff of his scent—earth and musk with a hint of soap. Axel always, and I mean always, smelled good. I wished I could smell as good as him.

"And?"

"I don't think she's the one we're looking for." My gaze landed on Forbes. He smacked his lips after taking a long sip of tea.

"I need more," he demanded.

"I really think I might throw something in his face before the night is over," I said.

Axel coughed into his hand to hide a chuckle. "You're probably not the only one thinking that."

Forbes cleared his throat and rested both hands on the gold-topped cane. "Do you want to hear my story?"

"If you're ready to tell it," Betty said.

The old man's eyes ticked around the room like the second hand of a clock. "I don't suppose any of you have ever had to outrun a magic eater?"

"No, and we already know that," Cordelia said impatiently. "We want to know what happened."

His eyes glittered with anger as they swept over Cordelia. Magnolia Cove's richest man did not like impudence.

Wow. I felt so smart using a word like *impudence*.

Forbes made sure not to look at Cordelia for the rest of the conversation. "I was alone in my house. I'd just heated up a can of soup and was about to eat it when the windows started quaking."

"So there was warning," CJ said. "Golly, I'm so glad there is. Can you imagine being asleep and this creature just appears and kills you?" CJ shivered. "Gives me the heebie-jeebies just thinking about it."

"I was annoyed if nothing else," Forbes said.

"Why does that not surprise me?" I murmured to Axel.

Forbes continued. "One of the windows exploded inside, sending glass shattering into my living room. That's when the creature entered. It was a hulking black mass, two hollow pits of hell for eyes and a mouth that was a tunnel that I knew would suck me dry. I called for my cane and created a holding spell. It wouldn't last long, I knew that. The magic eater's power would be too strong for it. But that spell gave me time to leave my house and flee here."

Betty pointed her pipe toward the door. "What was all that commotion when you arrived?"

"We thought he was the magic eater," Axel admitted sheepishly. "He showed up in a tunnel of power that whipped at the trees."

"I'm a powerful wizard," Forbes said with finality. "I can't help it that you're not used to seeing so much raw power."

I rolled my eyes. Boy, did this guy think a lot of himself.

"Do you think it followed you?" I asked.

"Do you hear it outside?" Forbes snipped.

I stared at Axel and shook my head, amazed at how rude this man could be. When I turned back to Forbes, I'd made sure to plaster a big smile on my face. "No, I don't hear it outside, but Sylvia had said before the creature snuck up quietly to her shop."

"Then she's deaf," Forbes snapped. "It's loud."

All gazes shot to Forbes. I was pretty sure at least one person wanted to spell his lips shut so he'd stop talking.

"If we want to survive," Forbes said, "we need to figure out a way to trick the magic eater back into the book. It might come here tonight. If it does, we need to be prepared."

"Smartest thing you've said," Betty replied. "Does anyone have an idea for that? Erebus won't go willingly. There's no telling how long he was trapped in the book in the first place. A little taste of freedom might be just what he's been waiting for."

"Sounds like he might go to the beach before he comes here," Amelia said. "Who could blame him? I'd rather be at the beach. The gulf is so nice this time of year."

"But it's always so crowded in the summer," Sylvia added. "It's best to go after school's back in session."

"That's true," Amelia replied.

Betty smacked the flat of her hand on the chair. "Will the two of y'all focus? We need to figure this out."

Cordelia threaded her fingers through her hair. "Why don't we just call him over to one of us and hide the book behind something? Then when he gets close, snap the book over him. Will that do it?"

Betty's lips coiled into a sly smile. "I think that just might work. Great thinking, Cordelia."

"Well, this is all my fault."

"No, it isn't," I snapped. "Someone slipped me the wrong spell." I didn't say it, but I was thinking that it was someone in the very room we all occupied.

Forbes spoke up. "Well, it wasn't me. I might be old, but I want to hang on to every bit of life I've got left. Even if I spend most of it heating up cans of soup to eat."

I didn't trust one crotchety word that leaped from Forbes's mouth. He was the guilty one who'd called down the magic eater. I was sure of it.

I considered his story and wondered if all of it was true. He said the window had broken and that he'd had soup. If the old man was telling the truth, the window would still be broken, wouldn't it? There would be irrefutable proof that Forbes's story was true.

I just wondered if there was a way for me to sneak out without anyone worrying.

After all, the magic eater wasn't interested in me.

"Pepper," Axel said in a low growl, "what are you thinking?"

I scowled. Figured Axel would catch me planning in my head. I scoffed as if the thought were ridiculous. "What makes you think I'm thinking anything?"

"You only get that look when you're up to something."

"I have no idea what you're talking about."

"Spill it."

I lowered my voice to a whisper. "I was just thinking that if what Forbes says is true, his window would be broken."

"And if it isn't, then he's lying."

"Right."

"And we could say he's the one who started this mess and force him to stop the magic eater."

"Right again." I smiled. "So what do you say? Think we can slip out and check?"

"No. We're needed here. What if the creature arrives?"

I nibbled my lower lip. It did sound horrible, leaving my family to investigate a house.

"We would be gone no more than five minutes. Couldn't you whisk us there with magic?"

"It would take a lot of magic."

"I'll do it. I need to practice traveling anyway. All we have to do is show up, check it out and return. Simple as that."

Worry filled his eyes. "What if something goes wrong? While we're out there?"

I linked my arm through Axel's and rested my head on his shoulder. "What could possibly go wrong? Erebus doesn't want us."

Axel's gaze scanned the room. "Fine. We go quickly and just see if his story is true. But we take someone else with us, just in case we need to get a message back here."

I could hardly contain my excitement at my victory. "Okay. We'll bring Hugo."

Axel shook his head. "No. If anything happens, Hugo will want to protect you. It'll put him in danger. The magic eater may attack."

"And the last thing we want to do is provoke it," I whispered.

"Right." Axel nodded toward Flower. "So I say we bring the possum. If anything happens, she can run back, tell everyone what happened."

I scanned the room of wide-awake witches and wizards, looking for a way to make our plan work. "Okay. Great idea."

"What are y'all two conspiring about over there?" Betty said.

I cringed.

Axel wrapped an arm around my shoulder. "We're discussing how to sneak away together and elope. Given all the drama going on, we figured it would be best to get married without anyone else around—in case something bad happened, that is."

"Can't say I blame you there," Cordelia said snidely. "That's what I would do if I were y'all."

Betty snorted. "No one's sneaking off anywhere."

We'd see about that. "Let me at least clean up." I crossed to Forbes, who sat with an empty cup of tea and bourbon resting on his lap. "Can I get you more?"

Forbes scowled. "No, I suppose not. Too much of that and I'll be blind drunk if the magic eater shows up again."

"We wouldn't want that," I mumbled. I took the rest of the empty cups, loaded them on the tray and headed into the kitchen.

"Flower, I could use some help in here."

The possum blinked at me before stretching and pawing her whiskers. "If you so say."

"I say so."

Betty shot me a hard look but said nothing. I grinned innocently, but I knew my grandmother wasn't buying it.

When I entered the kitchen, I settled the cups in the sink and turned around to see the possum giving me the stink eye. I wondered if she was taking lessons from Betty Craple.

"What do you need me to do? Wash? Dry?"

"I need you to come with Axel and me to Forbes Henry's house."

The possum arched a brow. "Tell me more."

As soon as I finished explaining the situation, Axel walked in.

"Do they suspect anything?" I said.

He nodded. "Oh yeah. Betty will probably walk in here any minute."

Speaking of the devil, the door opened and in sauntered my grandmother. She had a look so ferocious she could've given a lion a run for his money. She pulled her pipe from her mouth and blew a square of smoke.

"So you're going to Forbes," she stated.

I scoffed. "No idea what you're talking about."

"Can it," she said. "I'm coming too. The likelihood that the magic eater will hit the same place in one night is small. Let's go see if Forbes is telling the truth."

I shot Axel a knowing look. "Well, I say we go for it."

Axel nodded. "Hands together, y'all. Let's do this."

I closed my eyes, called on my magic and whisked us out into the night.

THE HOUSE WAS BLEAK. I mean seriously bleak. For all the money that Forbes Henry was supposed to have, his house certainly didn't look like it.

The old mansion had green moss growing on the roof. The black shutters were missing slats, and the shrubs were overgrown. A spot on my shoulders suddenly itched.

I told myself not to touch anything to avoid a staph infection.

"Don't touch anything," Betty grumbled.

Axel glanced around uneasily. "Let's go inside. I don't feel safe out here."

A wind ruffled Flower's fur. "Tell me about it."

"Storm's coming. Better to be inside than out here where we end up all wet." Betty clapped her hands, and the front doors opened.

We shuffled in. Lights buzzed and crackled to life as Betty snapped her fingers.

"Dining room should be easy to find," Betty said. "Follow me."

A staircase split the house in two. We followed Betty to the right and entered a parlor. The parlor led to a connected living room, and after that we entered the kitchen. An empty can of soup sat on the counter. Next we entered the dining room.

A mahogany table that easily seated twelve stretched in front of us. An empty bowl sat on the table. I peered into the room, searching for a broken window, but didn't find one.

I exchanged a glance with Betty and Axel. "No broken window."

Axel folded his arms, making his biceps bulge. A vein throbbed in his neck. "You know what that means."

"Forbes lied." Betty's lower lip trembled. "He's a nasty old coot, but I never expected that Forbes would call a magic eater to kill us off, one by one."

Fear spiked down my spine. "And now he's back at the house. We left our family alone with him." I grabbed Axel's hand. "We've got to get back there. Now!"

A door at the far end of the room banged open. I gasped and turned to see what could've caused such a sound.

Looming like a dark mist, Erebus drifted into the room, its sights set on Betty.

TEN

*T*he magic eater loomed like a black hole of energy, ready to suck the life from any and all of us. The creature had changed since I'd last seen it. The thing had a face that was oblong and reminded me of Edvard Munch's *The Scream*—an open void that would lead a person straight to the other side.

And not the good side.

Erebus's body was a sheet of mist curling at the floor and spreading out like the plague.

Terror, cold-filled terror hit me in my spine and slid to my gut. If Erebus's was the last face I saw before dying, someone would be in trouble because I'd be ticked off at that.

Like, I'd be so mad because his face was not a pretty one.

"Did anyone bring the book?" I said.

"No," Axel said, his voice tense.

"We really screwed up there," Betty added.

I stared at Axel and my grandmother in disbelief. "How could we have forgotten the book?"

"No one expected to see him, remember?" Betty said. "We didn't figure he'd be standing here waiting for us."

I stared as Erebus closed in on us. "We thought wrong."

"Please stop talking and get behind me," Axel said.

I flexed my fingers and splayed my legs in a fighting stance. "No way. You're not taking this thing on alone."

He flung out his arm. Axel was going to put me behind him one way or another. I wouldn't have it. But then I saw him yank a black pouch from his pocket and pull out a charcoal-gray looking powder.

He flung it at the magic eater and chanted something.

"You can't stand in my way," it hissed in a low, bone-chillingly even voice. It was like magic eating was simply part of its job. Just what it had to do in its daily life. Get up, drink some coffee, suck the life from someone—you know, totally routine.

No biggie, don't mind me while I eat this person's magic.

"You must leave," Axel demanded. "You can't have her today."

Erebus drifted forward. When he reached the spot where some of the powder lay on the carpet, the creature leaned over, and as delicately as a ballerina, it appeared to sniff the gray substance.

He jerked his head to Axel. "That won't stop me."

Axel folded his arms over his chest. "Then cross it."

Erebus took one step forward and screamed in pain. The magic eater jerked back. "You tricked me," he said accusingly.

"You saw what it was," Axel said. He fisted a handful of the powder from the pouch and heaved it back. "I said leave!"

Axel hurled it at Erebus. The creature's mouth opened grotesquely. The powder, which I now realized had small rocks in it, pelted him.

The magic eater howled in pain before vanishing into the night.

I released a low breath I hadn't realized I'd been holding and threw myself into Axel's arms. "It's gone, right?"

"For now," Axel said. "He'll be back tomorrow. I didn't buy us much time, but I did give us a little."

I released Axel and hugged Betty. "I'm so glad we're safe."

"Me too, kid," she said.

I gestured to Axel's pouch. "What is that?"

Axel closed the pouch and tucked it back in his pocket. "It's cremated happiness."

I squinted at him in confusion. "I'm sorry? Cremated happiness?"

Axel nodded. "It's happiness taken from children, made real and then cremated."

I jutted out my chin. "Were any children harmed in the making of that cremated happiness?"

He shook his head. "Don't worry. No children were harmed. The happiness was made into a clay figure and then pulverized. That's why there are so many large pieces. The only thing that was harmed was Erebus."

Betty adjusted her handbag on her arm. "And rightly so. Thank you for saving us, Axel. How did you ever happen to think that cremated happiness would work?"

He shrugged. "Something so evil would obviously be repelled by too much light."

"Well, I for one am glad you thought of it," Flower said. "Saved our rear ends."

Axel nodded. His jaw was clenched, and his eyes narrowed. "I only hope it works again. Magic eaters tend to learn and adapt."

I had to admit my hope sank when he said that.

Axel jerked his head. "Now about the broken window."

"To heck with the broken window," Betty said. "That creature was waiting for us. Pure and simple. Could've been coincidence, but as I don't see any broken glass, I don't think so."

I clenched my fists. "Forbes may as well have sent us here himself."

"Sent us to our deaths," Flower said.

Axel crossed to the table and inspected the rug underneath it. He knelt and ran his fingers atop the threads. "There isn't any glass on here, and if Forbes was as scared as he said he was, I doubt he would've taken the time to fix it before he left."

"And we know Erebus didn't fix it." I strode over to the huge lead-paned window and pressed my hand to one of the squares. "It's solid."

Betty cocked her chin. "It looks like Forbes has some explaining to do."

"Let me get us out of here." I crossed back to Axel, Betty and Flower. We joined hands, and I focused on whisking us back to the house.

I called on my magic, but nothing happened. No spark lit in my gut, and no spikes of energy zipped down my spine.

"We're ready, Pepper," Betty announced. "Take us back."

"I'm trying," I nearly growled in aggravation. "But it's not working."

Betty huffed in irritation. She puffed up her chest. "Hang on, I'll do it."

Even though I was slightly embarrassed at my magic for not wanting to work, I gave Betty an enthusiastic nod. "I must've used it all up when I transported us here."

"It's common for newbies to overuse their magic." Betty's grip on my hand tightened. "Hang on."

She grunted, which I knew to mean my grandmother was calling on her magic.

I waited, but we still stood in the middle of Forbes's dining room. "Hmm. Must be the stress," Betty mumbled. "My power doesn't seem to want to work, either."

Betty shot Axel a hopeful smile. "Will you do the honors?"

Axel scrubbed a hand down his cheek. "Of course. Hold tight."

He inhaled, his chest heaving, but once again nothing happened.

"We've been blocked," Axel announced.

I'd never heard that word before. "What do you mean, blocked?"

Betty dropped my hand. "He means our magic has been blocked from working."

"By who?"

Betty scowled. "I'll give you three guesses, and the first two don't count."

Forbes.

Panic clambered up my throat. I pushed it back down. I couldn't let negative emotions get the best of me. Not now. Not when danger lurked.

"So we can't get home?" I asked.

"We can't transport from in here," Axel explained. "But if we go outside, the situation might be different."

As much as I didn't want to leave the cover of the house, I knew it was the only option. I plucked Flower from the floor, tucked her under my arm, and we headed out.

Once we were clear of the home, we formed a ring and Axel tried to transport us again.

His chin set at an angle that suggested he was frustrated. "It still isn't working."

Betty spoke up. "Let me try."

She did but still nothing.

The wind howled. The storm was closing in on us. "What can we do?" I shouted above the rustling leaves and swaying branches.

"We're still blocked," Betty snarled. "All of us, I'd bet. We can't use our magic. At least not to transport. We'll have to walk back."

I balked. "Walk?"

Axel nodded. "The shortest way is through the Cobweb Forest."

"At night? Is that a good idea?"

Betty shouldered her purse and glared into the distance. "It's the best option we have."

"It's the only option." Axel pointed to the house. "I'll go back in and see if I can round up some flashlights."

The three of us waited outside until he returned. Luckily Axel managed to find exactly three torches to light our way.

We set off through the trees, keeping close together. Flower scurried at our feet, staying only a yard or two away at most.

"I feel so naked out here," I said.

Axel wrapped an arm around my shoulder. "We'll be okay. As scary as the Cobweb Forest is, it might be our best bet. If Erebus is able to get out from under the powder's hold before daylight, he would have a hard time tracking us in there. Too many other creatures to contend with."

Betty nodded. "The forest will protect us." She paused. "It also might kill us—we could run into something deadly. But I'm hoping things don't turn out that way."

Great. So now my emotions were stuck somewhere between relief and even greater anxiety.

"What about the storm?" I said the words, but as soon as our feet touched the layer of leaves that made up the forest bed, the wind died down.

"Things work differently here," Betty said.

"So I see."

The only sounds as we walked were our feet crunching on the leaves. I felt like an open target. The forest itself curled around us, the trees leaning in—or seeming to—cradling us as we walked.

Yet at the same time I felt like a sitting duck, simply waiting for the moment Erebus decided to appear from the mist.

A noise to my left made me jump. I glanced over to see a pine pull its roots from the ground and shuffle off to find a different location to drop its root bed down.

"Strange forest," Flower said.

I smirked. "You should be used to it. Aren't you from here?"

The possum hiked a shoulder. "Some things you never get used to."

I could understand that.

"Stay alert," Axel murmured. "If you see anything strange, let the rest of us know."

My jaw dropped. "Anything strange? Everything in this forest is strange."

Which was when a family of spiders the size of my fist traipsed right in front of us, crossing our path. They scurried along out of my flashlight's beam. I shined the flashlight on my face and shot Axel a pointed look that said, *See what I mean.*

His beam followed the spiders. "At least that seems normal compared to what else could be hiding in here."

The wind rustled the leaves, and a bad feeling crept over me like a blanket. "What if the trees move so much we can't find our way back? What if we end up lost in the forest?"

Betty tapped the butt of her flashlight. "It's got a compass. As long as we head due east, we should be fine."

"So I guess it's pretty obvious that Forbes set us up," I said.

Betty curled her fingers in front of her light. "As soon as we get back to the house, I'm going to wring his neck."

I stepped over a dead branch teeming with bugs. "But how could he have known someone would check the house?"

"I think he counted on his story raising suspicion," Axel said. "I only hope his plan wasn't to get rid of a few of us so that he could then hurt the others."

"He looks pretty frail," I argued. "I mean, what do y'all really think he's capable of?"

"Forbes Henry is rich and powerful—in magic, that is," Betty said. "Trust me, I know."

"So tell me the story—why did y'all think calling a blight down on Magnolia Cove would be good?"

"I want to know this, too." Axel swept his beam to the left and right. "I find it out of character for you, Betty."

She snorted. "There's no doubt I'm the pillar of perfection, but even the best of us stumble sometimes."

"Story," I demanded. "We've got time. Heck, we might have all night."

"We thought we were helping the town."

"Isn't that always how it is," I said.

Her gaze swept over my face as if to tell me, *Shut it.* When I made a motion that I was zipping my lips, Betty began.

"Magnolia Cove was in the middle of a drought. Snow said she had found an ancient spell to stop it, make the rains come. To this day I'm still not sure if she really knew what she was summoning or not. We didn't want to tell anyone what we were doing in case officials got angry, so we kept it a secret."

Betty huffed as we climbed a gradual slope. "We needed six and we had five people. Snow had a cousin, a young man with a lot of power."

"CJ Hix?" I said, still unable to believe that sweet, innocent CJ was capable of bringing any kind of blight to town. He was just too kind, too *golly gee, Miss Dunn,* for me to think anything bad of him.

And I definitely didn't think CJ had anything to do with the magic eater.

"CJ didn't know what he was getting involved in. Snow handled getting him to the meeting place, and we worked the spell. I heard the words and in that moment knew what Snow was calling forth wasn't rain—I knew it was evil, but we were too far along to stop."

She shuddered. "I remember catching eyes with Saltz Swift, and he had the same expression I had—we were doing something terribly, terribly wrong. A horrible thing would happen to our town and it did. The blight killed what crops were left and started to turn the drinking water sour.

"People were getting sick. We had to stop it. And we were all too afraid to tell anyone what we'd done. Poor CJ was a victim in all this, lassoed in. But in order to stop the terror that had plagued our town, we had to figure out a counter spell."

Betty stared blankly ahead. "Snow found it. Said what we had called was an actual spirit of blight. To stop it, the thing needed to be contained. We had to meet again. So we met and worked the new spell. The blight became something small and tangible—like an orb of fog. Snow took it and promised to dispose of it, send it back to the other world. Only one witch could do the final step, and we all trusted that it had been dealt with."

Betty didn't say anything else.

"Are you wondering if Snow really sent it back?"

Betty grimaced. Finally she shook her head. "How could she not have? Certainly we would've known if the blight hadn't been returned to where it came from."

"It would've come back," Axel said.

"That's what I believe," Betty replied.

A breeze whipped up the hair on the back of my neck. I hunched my shoulders and shivered. "But why would Forbes, after all this time, send a magic eater after you?"

Betty picked her way over a pile of twigs. "Maybe he doesn't want anyone to talk about what happened after he dies. No sullied reputation for Forbes, alive or dead."

"People have been killed for less," Axel said.

I supposed. "Maybe we shouldn't talk about these things in front of the possum. Right, Flower? You don't need to hear about this stuff."

Flower didn't answer.

I waved my beam across the ground. "Flower?" All I saw was a sea of leaves and trees. "Did any of y'all see what happened to her?"

Betty shook her head. "No."

"Me neither," Axel said.

Panic clambered up my throat. "But why? Where did she go? We can't leave her here. She's only a possum."

Betty placed a hand on my shoulder and squeezed. "I'm afraid we have to leave her."

"But—"

"No buts, Pepper," Betty snapped. "We've got to get home. Your cousins and our friends are alone with Forbes, a possible murderer."

And in that moment I knew Betty was right and I'd have to abandon Flower to survive in the Cobweb Forest, alone.

ELEVEN

$\mathcal{W}$e reached the house at daybreak. I was sore, tired and ready to fall into my bed.

But there was no rest for any of us. The first thing we had to do was deal with Forbes.

As soon as we stepped inside, Betty pinned her steely gaze on the old man, pointed her finger at him and declared, "We went to your house. The window wasn't broken, and Erebus was waiting for us."

Forbes's mouth went slack. "Did you really think I would leave my house with a shattered window?" he said snottily. "I fixed it before leaving."

Betty shot Garrick a hard look. The sheriff ran a hand down his face. "Let me get this straight—you were under attack from a magic eater that broke your window, and you took the time to then fix said window before fleeing."

"Obviously," Forbes said.

But Betty wasn't letting that excuse gain any traction. "Plus our magic was blocked. We got rid of the magic eater—for now—but we had to walk back here. That's why we're only arriving now."

Forbes glared at Betty. "Why don't you just go ahead and say what you want to say?"

"Okay, Mr. Henry, I'll say it—you summoned that magic eater to kill us. I want you arrested for murder and attempted murder."

Forbes's face paled. He whirled on Garrick. "You're not going to let this crazy woman talk like this about me, are you?"

"I'm not crazy. I'm the most sane person here," Betty countered.

Garrick studied Forbes before dragging his gaze to Axel. "Can you corroborate this?"

Axel nodded. "Everything was as Betty said."

Garrick slowly rose from his seat in the recliner. He stretched his legs and reached his hands over his head to work the kinks from his body. Then Garrick pulled a pair of handcuffs from his back pocket.

"Why don't you come down with me to the station, Mr. Henry?"

"I will not," Forbes said tightly. "I will not go anywhere with you because I am innocent."

Garrick took a step forward. "Why don't we talk about it?"

"I have nothing to discuss."

Garrick took another step forward, and I can't be sure of what exactly went through Forbes's mind but his expression was a mixture of caged rat and cornered lion.

Garrick took one more step. "Just come talk."

That was when Forbes cocked his hand back and let it fly forward, hitting Garrick smack on the chin. A loud crack sounded, and Garrick's head snapped back.

Everything stopped. The air was sucked from the room.

Amelia spoke, saying what I'm pretty sure all of us were thinking. "That was a bad idea."

Garrick slowly lowered his head. Rage burned in his eyes. He leveled his gaze at Forbes and said in a low voice, one filled with more anger than I knew Garrick was capable of, "You are coming with me."

Forbes shook his head. "I can't. I can't come with you."

"You just hit an officer of the law."

"To save myself," Forbes pleaded. "You don't understand. If I come with you, I'll be dead. The magic eater will get me. There'll be no escape."

"You should've thought about that before you hit him," Amelia scolded.

Garrick shot her a dark look.

"Sorry," she whimpered.

Garrick placed a hand on Forbes and pulled him forward. "Now. You'll need to come with me."

The old man clutched Garrick. "Please. You can't take me. I'm sorry I hit you. I know my house looks bad, but I have nothing to do with this Erebus."

"We can discuss it at the station," Garrick said calmly.

Forbes's grip tightened, but Garrick managed to get the handcuffs on him. The officer placed a hand on Forbes's shoulder and heaved him toward the door.

"Please," Forbes repeated, "I know things about the magic eater. A way to stop it. I can help. I promise I can. I'm not lying. You have to believe me..."

Axel held the door open, and Garrick pulled Forbes through. Betty placed a finger to her nostril, and a line of magic zipped from her nose, slamming the door shut.

"Good riddance," she griped.

I nibbled my bottom lip. "He said he knew something that would help us."

"Probably lies," Betty said. She raked her fingers down her face and collapsed onto a chair. "How about we all get a little rest and then come up with a plan? Erebus's power is stronger at night than it is during the day. I'm thinking he'll stay away for a while."

"Yeah," Amelia seconded. "Y'all look like you spent all night walking through the Cobweb Forest."

"We did," Betty snapped. "I thought we already told you that."

"You did," Amelia whimpered. "I just thought I'd reiterate it."

Suddenly the long night caught up with me. Every muscle in my legs hurt, my head swam from fatigue and I could barely keep my eyes open.

I stifled a yawn. "I'm going upstairs."

Axel caught my gaze. "I'll head home for a while. Come back at lunch. Unless anyone thinks they're going to need me."

"We'll be okay," Betty said.

CJ Hix rose. "That's right, Mr. Reign. I got a good night's sleep. I should be able to help however I can if something happens. Not that I think it will, but golly, I'm here and I'm an able-bodied man."

Humor flashed in Axel's eyes. I shot him a quick grin before climbing the stairs to my bedroom and collapsing on my bed.

Sleep overtook me as soon as I got my second sneaker off.

I awoke to a wet tongue licking my cheek. I blinked my eyes open to find Hugo, tongue lolled to one side, staring at me.

"Come here, boy. I've missed you."

Hugo jumped on the bed, and I pulled him into a cuddle. The once-baby dragon was almost too large to cuddle, but I made it work. All I had to do was wrap one arm around his middle. We lay there for a moment until I realized there was a ton of work to be done.

We had to figure out a way to trick Erebus into going back into the book.

But how?

I jumped from the bed, nearly trampling Mattie the Cat on my way to the bathroom.

"Sugar, I don't see no fire," she said through a yawn.

"There's a magic eater trying to kill Betty. If that's not a fire, I don't know what is."

Mattie bowed her back and stretched out her claws. "Well, why didn't you say so? Get on with your bad self."

I quickly showered, changed and tromped downstairs to find all heck breaking loose.

Mint and Licky stood in the middle of the living room, arguing with Betty.

"But we want to help," Mint said.

"We want to make it up to you," Licky said.

Betty tapped a wooden spoon on the rim of the cauldron bubbling over the everlasting fire. "Y'all have done enough. If you hadn't accepted that invitation from Snow to join the group, none of this would've happened in the first place."

Sylvia Spirits glanced away from a book she had propped on the dining table. "Maybe you should listen to them. It can't hurt."

Betty's face turned rose-red. "Can't hurt? These two chaos witches will end up calling Erebus here and handing us over to him one at a time."

Mint fisted a hand to her hip. "We aren't going to do that, Mama. We've been researching ways to trick the magic eater back into his book."

Licky stepped forward. "We have a plan. All you have to do is listen to us."

"Could be worth a shot," CJ said. "Gosh, I don't want to die for some accident I did years ago. And I don't want the good people of Magnolia Cove to suffer for me, either."

Betty relented. "Fine. What have you got for us?"

Mint and Licky shot each other a victorious look. They hovered around Betty.

"We were reading up on ways to attract a magic eater," Mint said.

"When we had the idea that maybe there was something out there that would lure it in," Licky added.

Mint nodded her head. "Like sort of what the insect world does."

"The predators, she means," Licky clarified.

Betty shook her head. "Will the two of y'all *not* speak at the same time and go slow. You're making my noggin buzz."

Mint took a deep cleansing breath. "In the insect world predators are oftentimes very flashy looking to attract their prey."

"Like a Venus flytrap," Licky said. "The plant looks like something a fly might like to eat. The fly thinks the flower is something it wants."

"But then the fly ends up dead," Mint added on. "Once the fly is close enough, the flower traps it and slowly eats it."

"I ain't eating no magic eater," Betty snapped.

Mint's eyes glittered with intelligence. "You don't have to. We created something that will help. Something we think will attract Erebus and can be used to get him back in the book."

Betty paused. I could tell she was dying to know but at the same time was afraid to ask. Mint and Licky's plans backfired more often than not.

To be honest, I was afraid too, but we needed all the help we could get.

"What do you have?" I asked.

Mint tapped her fingers together with glee. "Now, it took some time to figure this out, but what Erebus wants more than anything is magic—to eat it, right?"

"Specific magic," Betty said. "He was sent here for us." She nodded toward Sylvia and CJ.

"That's what got us thinking." Licky dragged a finger down one side of her mouth. "We thought that he wants specific people."

Mint tag teamed her sister. "So no regular magic will do."

"Right." Licky's gaze flashed from Betty to the rest of us in the room. "So if we baited Erebus with Pepper's magic, for instance, it wouldn't work."

"What wouldn't work?" Betty asked impatiently.

"This." From her pocket Mint pulled a golden dogwood flower.

I peered closer. "What is that?"

"It's a pin for your blouse," Betty said, unimpressed.

Licky poked the air with authority. "But under the right conditions, this golden flower could be more. If we seeded it with bits of y'all's magic—a little of Sylvia's, some of CJ's and a teensy bit of Betty's, the magic eater might find himself attracted to it."

My eyes widened as I realized their plan. "And then if you placed the flower near the book, or even on the book, Erebus might not pay attention. He'd be so interested in the power residue he might just fall back into the book—being tricked by your plan."

Mint clapped her hands. "Bingo! You've got it."

Licky eyed me proudly. "You are one smart niece." She turned to Betty. "Mama, do you think it'll work?"

Betty rubbed her chin as she stared at Sylvia and then CJ. "Hard to say. It would take an awful lot of magic to charge up such an object."

"But it can be done," Sylvia said.

CJ brushed lint from his pants. "I'm game if y'all are. Heck, we've got nothing to lose. Unless Garrick gets a confession out of Forbes and forces him to call off the magic eater, we don't have a better option."

"And the sun is already beginning to set," Sylvia said. "It'll be night soon, and he'll be powering up, ready to come for us."

Betty's expression was grim. "So I guess we don't have another choice."

"We've thought about it a lot," Mint said soothingly.

Licky nodded enthusiastically. "It should work."

"Unless it doesn't," Amelia said.

Betty shot her a dark look. "It's as good an option as we have." She squinted her eyes and glared at Licky and Mint. "Let's get started."

TWELVE

I left Mint, Licky and everyone else at the house and decided to go out and enjoy the little bit of sun we had until night fell.

The streets were deathly quiet. All I could hear was the wind howling. Betty had mentioned that people already knew about the magic eater and were holing themselves in their homes.

I believed it went beyond that. People knew *who* Erebus was after. They didn't want to run into him, which was why many were still staying in town, but they also knew they were safe from him—at least for now.

Axel called while I was out. "You okay?"

I glanced around as if I wasn't supposed to be okay. "Yes, I'm fine."

"Where are you?"

I told him I was near Bubbling Cauldron, not far from downtown.

"Wait there for me. I'll be by soon."

"I'm totally safe. The magic eater hopefully won't be back until nightfall."

He huffed. "I'd rather you not walk alone."

"Fine.

I found a bench and sat, waiting for Axel. A few minutes later he rolled up in his Land Rover and parked. Axel buzzed down the passenger window. "I'll get out. We can walk."

"What are we doing?"

"Keeping an eye out."

"For the magic eater?"

He nodded. "That's right." Axel's blue eyes scanned the street. "If we can find it before it finds Betty, we have a better chance of beating it."

Axel buzzed the window back up and got out.

The idea mystified me. We were tracking something that was nothing more than mist, and we were simply going to walk on two legs instead of driving?

Strange.

Axel raked his hair from his eyes. "We can sense it better if there's nothing between it and us. Besides"—he flashed me a smile—"it gives us a chance to talk."

Even though we were under a stressful situation, Axel still threaded his fingers through mine and kissed the back of my hand.

"Things might be stressful, but we can still find five minutes to enjoy *us*."

I smiled brightly, feeling my body shine from the inside out. "There are times when I wish the entire world could feel this way."

Axel smiled sadly. "And then you remember that there are murderers and innocent people die."

My smile faded. "Yeah, that would be it." I paused. "Wouldn't it be weird if the magic eater had his own family? What if he was trapped in the book, chained against his will, and all he wanted was to just return to his own Betty Craple?"

Axel laughed. "His own Betty Craple? Are you sure he'd want to return at all?"

It was my turn to chuckle. I elbowed him in the ribs. "He would want to get back to his family. Of course he would. That's what life is all about—family."

"And becoming one." Axel eyed me knowingly. "Like I want us to become family."

"Which we are—we just have to find the right spot."

He shook his head and sighed. "I know you want a barn wedding, but you know we could create a barn right here." Axel pointed to the park by Bubbling Cauldron. "Build it and instead of hanging lights, we can hire fairies to light the night. See if Garrick will suspend some of the rules on only witches being allowed into town and have a lot of other creatures."

I smirked. "I don't want anyone to bend the rules for me."

"You helped save this town and change the Head Witch Order." He tapped my nose. "You, Pepper Dunn. I'm pretty sure the town would have no problem helping us out."

It just didn't seem right to take advantage of my place in Magnolia Cove. I hadn't stopped the Head Witch Order on purpose. The whole situation had come about because I was trying to figure out how to stay alive.

I linked my arm through his. "I'd feel better if we married in a small town where all creatures are allowed. Or even if we got married in a cornfield—as long as werewolves will be allowed same as witches, I'm all for it."

Axel stopped and turned to me. I raised my chin, and he brushed a strand of honey-colored hair from my eyes. "Thank you. That hair was really annoying me."

"It looked like it," he murmured before gently kissing me.

A spark lit in my core, and I sighed into the kiss, letting my body press against him.

When we parted, Axel whispered, "I don't care where we marry. As long as we're together, that's all that matters."

I grinned. "I agree."

Axel jerked his head toward the street. "Come on. Let's see if we can ferret out Erebus."

But finding the magic eater turned out to be more difficult than we had originally hoped. There were no signs of him anywhere—I mean, if you call signs things like shattered glass and uprooted trees, that was.

And I did. Knowing the amount of destruction Erebus was capable of, I figured he would leave a trail of destruction in his wake.

But there was no trail.

Not even leading up to Snow's house. Erebus had started at our house and then ended up at Snow's without anything in between being ripped up.

I asked Axel why that was.

He shrugged. "Probably because he didn't need to destroy anything because there wasn't a person he was targeting between your house and Snow's."

"But Betty lives at the house."

Axel shrugged. "He went for Snow first."

"But why?"

"Because that's where Forbes sent him."

I trudged up a grassy slope on the other side of the park and came to a stop underneath a tall pine. I plucked a dead needle from the grass and twirled it between my thumb and forefinger.

"Yeah, you're probably right," I finally said.

We watched the sun burn down the horizon in silence until Axel finally turned to me. "Ready to get back?"

I nodded. "Yep. We're setting a trap to get Erebus back in the book. Mint and Licky are in charge."

Axel shot me a concerned look. "And Betty's allowing this?"

"I don't think she knows what else to do."

Axel ran a thumb down his jawline. "Let's get back—make sure Mint and Licky haven't screwed anything up."

Just then my phone rang. I slid it from my pocket and glanced down. "It's Cordelia." I grimaced. A knot twisted my gut.

"Answer it," Axel said. "I'm sure it's bad."

Praying that whatever Cordelia said couldn't be that horrible, I thumbed the Answer button and pressed the phone to my ear.

"Hey. Everything okay?"

"Pepper, you've got to get back here."

Okay, so if I had to take a gander, I would say that no, everything was not okay.

"What happened?"

"I don't know. I just got home and can't find anybody. But when I call for them, I can hear their voices, but I don't see them."

I cringed. "Your mother and aunt were there working a spell that they thought would save Betty and the rest from Erebus."

Cordelia groaned. "But no one's here."

"Yet you hear them?"

"Yes!"

I shot Axel a worried look. Dread washed over me like cold water from a showerhead. I closed my eyes and pulled in my lips in frustration. "Do me a favor and look around. See if you can find a small gold dogwood pin. The sort old ladies wear on their blouses."

"What's wrong?" Axel asked.

I placed a hand over the mouthpiece. "Cordelia can't find them, but she can hear everyone."

"Think Mint and Licky whisked them away to another dimension?"

I shot Axel a harsh look for even suggesting such a thing. Though I had to admit I was worried a little bit of a *Stranger Things* was going on.

I prayed it wasn't.

"I found the pin," Cordelia said. Her breathing came hard. My cousin was panting she was so worried.

"Take a close look at it. What do you see?"

Cordelia gasped. "Oh no! I dropped the pin."

I heard a muffled sound while I assumed my cousin scrambled to pick up the pin. A moment later Cordelia returned, huffing.

"You're never going to believe this," she said.

I seriously doubted that. Whenever Mint and Licky were involved in something, I was pretty sure I would believe whatever the outcome.

"What is it?" I finally asked.

When Cordelia spoke, her voice shook. "I found our family and then some."

I squeezed my lids tight, hoping the answer would be different from what I expected. "Where are they?"

Cordelia clicked her tongue. "They're trapped in this old lady pin."

I groaned. "That's what I was afraid of."

"What?" Axel said.

I sighed and dropped the phone to my chest. "Like all things that go wrong when Mint and Licky are involved, it appears that their plan to saturate a pin with Betty's, Sylvia's and CJ's powers has gone terribly wrong."

He groaned. Even Axel knew what I was about to say was bad. "Let me guess? Everything backfired and they're now trapped in the pin."

"You guessed it." I put the phone back to my mouth. "Cord, hang on. We'll be there in a minute to get this straightened out."

No sooner had I hung up than Axel and I were back at the Land Rover and then at the house, barging in to attempt to save the day.

We found Cordelia pacing the living room.

I could hear my grandmother's shouting as soon as we entered. "Get us out of here!"

Cordelia pointed to it. "There it is."

Axel and I rushed over, and the three of us hovered around the pin. The glossy gold surface reflected the light, but inside I could see them —tiny little Mint, Licky, Amelia, Betty, CJ and Sylvia.

"Help us," Mint called.

Betty elbowed her in the ribs. "It's because of y'all that we're in this mess!"

"We were only trying to help," Licky said.

Amelia leaped forward. "Please! It's so hot and cramped in here. I can't take it!"

"We need to get them out before they kill each other," I murmured.

Cordelia smirked. "Do we really have to? I've got dibs that Betty survives the longest."

I stifled a laugh behind my hand.

"What's so funny?" Betty demanded.

"Nothing." I waved away her concern. "I'm going to let Axel help y'all. Cordelia and I are going to step over here for a minute."

"All right," Axel said, taking control. "One at a time, tell me what happened."

Everyone started yelling at once.

"That's why I wanted to walk over here." I pulled Cordelia over to the fire. "I knew they wouldn't be able to talk quietly about it."

Cordelia raked her fingers through her hair. "What a mess."

"Does Garrick have any ideas how to stop the magic eater?"

She shook her head. "He's relying on us for that." My cousin dropped her voice. "And he's considering charging Betty, CJ and Sylvia with a crime."

I grasped her arm. "Why them?"

"Because in some ways this is all their fault." Sadness filled her eyes. "If it hadn't been for Betty and them and that stupid blight, none of this would've happened. We don't know that Erebus will leave once he's taken their magic. What if he stays?"

I nibbled my bottom lip. "You're right. I can understand Garrick's position. But if he was going to arrest anyone, I would think it'd be us —we're the ones who released the magic eater."

"We were tricked," Cordelia said.

"We never should've worked the spell to begin with," I argued. "We didn't need it."

"I needed it," she said harshly. "We were drowning in mason jars. It was so stupid of me, so stupid to push us into something we never should've done."

I studied her for a moment, trying to figure out where her newfound anger was coming from. "You're really taking this out on yourself, aren't you?"

Cordelia dropped her chin to her chest. "If Garrick was going to arrest anyone, it should be me. It's my fault that all of this happened."

I shook my head. "It wasn't just you. It was the three of us. Cordelia…"

She wasn't listening. Cordelia stared out the window as the sun burned away. "Once this is over, I'm going to demand Garrick charge me with a crime." Her gaze locked on mine. Tears watered her eyes.

"All of this is my fault, and because of that, I'm going to make sure Garrick arrests me for magical neglect."

I gasped. "But magical neglect means you'll spend time in jail."

Cordelia nodded. "I deserve it. This whole mess is my fault, Pepper. It's mine and I have to pay for it."

THIRTEEN

$\mathcal{I}$ was about to tell Cordelia that her idea of being charged with a crime and taking on all the guilt of what had happened was a horrible one when Axel called us back over.

"I can get them out," he explained by the window so none of them could hear. "It's a simple reversal spell. It won't take much time or effort, but…"

I rubbed my lips together as his unsaid idea planted a seed of interest in my brain. "But you're wondering if it's better to leave them inside."

"At least for tonight," he said. Axel folded his arms and ran a hand down the stubble sprouting from his cheeks. "Erebus won't be able to get at them. It would be impossible. But he might be drawn here."

My eyelids flared in excitement. "And that would give us a chance to catch him."

"Exactly." Axel grinned. "Great minds do think alike."

"Great minds that are meant to be together," I said.

His smile deepened before fading. "But that means we have to come up with a plan."

I jerked my thumb toward the pin. "Will they be okay in there?

Amelia said it was hot. Do they have enough oxygen? What about food and water?"

"I'll take them food," Cordelia offered. "I can go in. I'll take personal fans, too. The kind with misters if they need them."

Axel nodded. "They should have plenty of air. They're not that big."

"What are y'all talking about?" Betty's tinny-sounding voice demanded. "We want out."

I shot Axel an encouraging look. "Are you going to break the news to them?"

He set his chin in a determined line. "I'll do it. Betty will understand."

I patted his back. "I hope she doesn't hate you for the rest of your life."

He shot me a surprised look, and then after seeing the mischievous grin on my face, Axel relaxed. "Here goes nothing."

I patted his shoulder. "We'll do it together."

Needless to say our offer to allow Betty and the gang to remain in the pin for one night was met with serious protests. We did our best to explain the situation to my family and friends that this would be the best thing to do—at least for one night.

After about ten minutes of arguing, they finally relented.

"We're sending Cordelia in with supplies," I explained.

"What about a john?" Betty said. "We're going to need one of those, too."

Axel swooped in to the rescue. "I'll send one there. How's that?"

Betty worked her bottom lip. She was ticked, I could tell. But my grandmother also knew this was the best thing to do under the circumstances.

"I guess it'll do," she finally snarled.

Axel nodded to Cordelia, who wore a backpack full of supplies. "Let's do this."

Once Cordelia was all settled into the pin, Axel and I set about coming up with a plan.

We hashed it out over the dining room table while we each drank a glass of sweet tea. After we'd gone over it several times, I finally glanced up from the piece of paper filled with pencil marks.

I smiled. "I think it's brilliant. This should work."

Axel nodded. "If it doesn't, we're screwed."

I shot him a scathing look. "Don't say that. No matter what, we're not screwed. We will find a way."

He exhaled and leaned back in his chair, stretching his arms. "You're right. There's always a way."

I glanced at the window. The last smears of orange and pink were fading on our walls. Darkness would be here soon, and hopefully so would Erebus.

I clenched my fists. I was ready for the magic eater to bring on everything he had.

I felt my lips coil into a devilish smile. "Let's do this."

AXEL HELD the book between his hands. I sat behind a five-foot mirror, ready for Erebus.

The mirror will help to confuse him, Axel had explained. *I know it sounds strange, but we need Erebus not to think too much.*

This had to go fast, and it was as tricky as pulling a tick off a dog's chin.

"What if he doesn't show?" I said in a hushed voice. "What if he goes to the jail instead?"

Axel shrugged. "That won't happen. If Forbes is the one controlling him, which we both believe, the magic eater will appear here."

I bit the inside of my mouth. "Do you remember what Forbes said about having inside knowledge of Erebus?"

Axel nodded.

"What do you think he meant?"

"I think he was bluffing," Axel said curtly. "It was just a way to stop Garrick from arresting him."

"Didn't work."

"Not when you punch a cop, it won't."

I was about to ask something else about Forbes when the door blew smack open. The sound startled me. I jumped from behind the mirror and caught a glance at Erebus.

The magic eater's mist nearly ate the room it spread so far out away from him. Erebus fixed his gaze on Axel.

"They're not here," Axel said. "Your magic detector isn't working right."

Erebus drifted forward and stopped in front of Axel.

Axel eyed him nonchalantly. "They're not here."

Erebus cocked his head like a dog questioning something his master has said. Axel shrugged.

Erebus extended a long, wispy arm and reached.

In the blink of an eye, Axel raised the pin into the air. "Pepper!"

I rose. Axel tossed the pin to me. I had to get this right. Had to catch it. I opened my palm, and the golden pin landed safely inside.

Erebus whirled toward me. I stared down the magic eater as he lunged toward the mirror.

I had to hold my position. Had to let Erebus get as close as possible before making another move.

As his long spindly arm came toward me, I had to bank on two things—the first was that Erebus wouldn't attack and the second was that I could make a three-point shot.

"Axel!"

I tossed the pin back to Axel, who caught it one-handed. He opened the book and tucked the pin into the middle crease.

I swear Erebus glared at me before spinning around. The creature leaped forward, and Axel held open the book, counting on the fact that Erebus would be more focused on his prey than what he was actually doing.

Erebus zipped through the air and dived headfirst into the pages of the book he had come from.

The magic eater had disappeared from sight. My jaw dropped. My heart pounded against my chest. I took a deep gulp of air.

Axel laid one hand flat on the book and chanted low. He exhaled a deep breath and flashed me a victorious smile. "It worked. Erebus entered the book."

I reached for Axel. "We did it! We stopped him!"

Axel pulled me into a hug. I relaxed into him, relieved that the entire ordeal was over. After a moment I could hear Betty starting to yell at us again.

"Is it done? Get us out of here," she demanded.

Axel released me and rolled his eyes. "Yes, ma'am. Let's get you out of there."

Axel opened his hand. The pin still lay in his palm. He waved another hand over it and started to chant when a rumble filled the house.

I glanced over to the book that Axel had laid on the couch. My eyelids flared as it rattled and shook.

"Um. Axel." I pointed to it. "I think we have a problem."

The book burst open. Pages flipped on an invisible current. My stomach clenched.

"Uh-oh." I grabbed Axel's sleeve. "We'd better get out of here!"

"Betty, we'll have to save you later." He slipped the pin into his pocket. "Run!"

We raced to the front door just as a loud screech filled the air. I glanced over my shoulder to see Erebus stretching up to the ceiling, fully formed, his escape complete.

What had gone wrong? We got him back into the book. How could we have screwed up?

There was no time to think about it. There was only time to focus on survival. I dashed out into the night, following Axel.

"Grab my arm," he shouted.

I took hold of him. A flash of light and a popping sound filled the air. A moment later Axel had magicked us away from Betty's house.

We stood on the bank of the Potion Ponds. The humid night air made my skin immediately break into a sweat. The hair at the back of my neck clung to my flesh. I pulled it over my shoulder, hoping it would help me cool off.

I turned to Axel. "What happened? Why didn't Erebus stay in the book?" I threw my arms into the air. "We did what we were supposed to. We tricked him. He went in. How the heck could he get out?"

Axel hung his head. "I don't know."

I groaned. "This just gets worse and worse."

"At some point it'll get better," Axel said. "You have to believe me."

I gave him a wobbly smile. "I believe you. It's just so much—we can't get any relief from this guy."

A rustle of leaves behind us made me turn. "What is that?" Even as the word left my mouth, a feeling of dread washed down my skin, pricking my flesh inch by inch.

"It can't be," Axel said in a low voice.

"It can't be what?" *Please don't say it's the magic eater.*

The tree branches parted, and out into the night rolled Erebus.

"It's the magic eater," Axel said, mystified. He threw his arms out protectively. "Stay back. Get behind me."

"We can both hit him with our power," I argued.

"He eats power, Pepper," Axel snapped. "It won't do any good."

I grimaced. Wow. How could I not have been on top of that one? Fighting a magic eater with magic was like fighting a forest fire with more fire—it simply wouldn't work.

Axel pulled the black pouch full of happiness from his pocket. "Stay back, Erebus," he warned.

But Erebus either didn't listen or didn't care. My vote would be that the magic eater didn't care. The creature glided forward. Axel threw a handful of powder at the ground and on Erebus.

He slowed for a moment, bowing his back. Then the magic eater shook off the cremated gunk and advanced on us again.

I clutched Axel's shirt. "What happened?"

"He got an immunity." Axel tugged me toward him. "Run!"

We ran toward the ponds. Axel shouted at me. "We're going to dive in."

I looked at him as if he was crazy. "What?"

"Dive in," he repeated.

"What if Erebus isn't afraid of water?"

"That won't matter." Axel shot me a frantic look. "Do you trust me?"

"Yes!"

"Then do as I say. Dive in." We were almost to the edge. I'd never once been in the sparkling water of the Potion Ponds. Not once had I seen anyone swim in them, and though they looked like diamonds on the surface, there was no telling what lay underneath.

This was the South, y'all. There could be all kinds of cottonmouths in the water. It was always best to be a little fearful, at least when deadly creatures were involved.

"Now," Axel shouted.

I launched myself into the air. My feet lifted from the ground as I tucked my head and brought my arms up to both ears.

Once you learn to dive, it's like riding a bike—you never forget.

My fingers touched the cool water first. I sliced through the surface, feeling the rest of my body plunge into the pond.

I kicked as I held my breath. I opened my eyes. The water was dark —no surprise there, as it was dark outside. As my vision adjusted, I realized we were in deep water. Tall lake weed that was anchored to the pond floor drifted around us.

The sparkling lights that always danced on the surface of the pond lit up in the distance, reminding me of fireflies. They looked so beautiful as they approached. I extended my hand toward one of them.

A tiny body flitted toward me. It looked like a small fairy with big eyes and a face that held nothing but goodness and generosity. The little light fairy flicked her wings and sailed in the water.

I smiled, reaching my hand out to touch her. The small fairy's mouth opened into what I had originally thought was a smile, but then large piranha-like teeth flashed before me.

I released my lungs just as Axel's hand wrapped around my wrist. I turned toward him, and in another flash and a pop, we were gone from the ponds.

I lay soaking on the ground. Water had entered my lungs. I heaved it up, vomiting it onto the gravel.

Axel coughed and sputtered beside me. My lungs burned, and my chest ached.

I reached for him. He grabbed my hand and placed it on his chest. A dim light flared close by. I peeled my eyes open, forcing myself to see what the light was.

"It'll hurt for a minute," Axel explained. "It's way too easy to get used to the ponds once you're underwater. That's what they want you to do."

"Who?"

"The sprites in there. They're not always active, but when they are, they're ferocious little beasts. I'm hoping they keep Erebus busy for a while."

I coughed again. "Did he jump in?"

Axel nodded. "I think so. I felt the water quake just before we left. Joke's on him. The sprites swarm."

I pushed a strand of hair that was plastered to my forehead away. "Why do they do that?"

Axel winked at me. "Because they like to taste invaders." He pushed himself from the ground. Water dripped from his clothes, pooling at his feet.

He extended a hand toward me and grinned. "That's why I grabbed you before you got too close. Trust me. I did you a favor."

I slid my palm over his and let Axel pull me to my feet. "Why's that?"

"Sweetheart, if they'd gotten a taste of you, I'm pretty sure those sprites wouldn't have stopped tasting. You'd be their next meal."

FOURTEEN

etween my family being stuck in an old lady's pin, facing off against flesh-eating sprites and encountering one ticked-off magic eater, this had been one heck of a night.

The lights stung my eyes. I covered them. "Where are we?"

Axel's hand steadied me. "Take it slow. Give yourself a moment. Being in the ponds can screw with your sight."

"But where are we?"

"The police station."

"Why?"

"In case Erebus shows back up."

I blinked. My eyes were now adjusting to the light. Axel pressed his fingers into the small of my back. "Come on. Let's get inside and take cover."

I stumbled into the police station. My legs were weak, and I shook from the adrenaline coursing through me. Let's face it—I was seriously in fight-or-flight mode. My tongue felt like sandpaper, and every outside movement made me jump.

"Garrick," Axel shouted. "We've got issues."

Garrick charged out from his office. "What now?"

Axel explained the situation—everything from the pin to Erebus and the failed attempt to get him into the book.

Garrick shifted his weight and scratched his chin. "Well, now what do we do?"

"I told y'all that I knew things about the magic eater—things y'all would need from me."

The voice of a haggard old man drifted out from one of the cells. Every head snapped in his direction.

Feet shuffled and a moment later Forbes stood before us, his arms linked through the bars. "Well, well, well. Now it looks like y'all need the innocent old man you locked up."

"You assaulted me," Garrick snapped.

Forbes studied his fingernails. "I'm old and fearful. When you get to be my age, you'll understand."

I rolled my eyes.

"Erebus might be on his way here," Axel said quickly. "We left him at the Potion Ponds, but he tracked us there. There's no telling if he'll be able to find us here."

"So whatever we're going to do, we need to do it fast," I added.

Garrick raised his hands. The doors locked. He pointed to the windows, and their locks snapped as well.

"Wasting your time," Forbes mumbled. "Remember, he broke my window. Locks won't stop Erebus."

"Do you have a better idea?" I snapped. "It's one thing to offer suggestions and it's quite another to stand there and taunt us." I pointed my finger at Forbes. "He's coming for you, you know. You're a sitting duck."

I folded my arms and glared at him. "Unless of course, you're the one who had us summon him to begin with."

Forbes snarled. "It wasn't me. I've already explained that."

I shot Axel and Garrick a concerned look. "Well?"

"We may not have a choice," Axel said. "At least for tonight we should listen to him."

"You have to let me out," Forbes said. "You'll have to get me out of this cell. Inside here I'm a sitting duck, especially if everyone else is stuck inside a pin."

Garrick's jaw clenched. "Only in exchange for your help."

Sweat sprinkled Forbes's forehead. His hands tightened on the cell bars. "Yes. Only in exchange for that. I understand. Please! If the magic eater appears, there'll be no escape."

Garrick rushed to Forbes and unlocked the cell. Forbes stumbled from his cage, and Garrick caught the old man in his arms.

"Thank you," Forbes gasped. "Thank you for letting me out."

Garrick steadied him until Forbes found his footing. "What do you know about the magic eater?"

Forbes's eyes sparkled with intelligence. I got the feeling the old coot liked it when he had all the power.

"I heard that you weren't able to get him inside the book, huh?" he directed to Axel.

Axel folded his arms. "How does that help us now?"

"Because tricking him isn't good enough. That's what everyone thinks—you have to trick a magic eater into returning to the book— but that isn't true. He's got a purpose, hired by someone to destroy several of us. First, we don't know who gave you the incantation to call him. You, Pepper Dunn, and your cousins summoned him, but it was at the will of someone else."

Forbes took a breath. "It makes this more challenging. The first thing we have to know is who originally requested Erebus. The name would be in the spell. Do you have the original spell you used?"

My mind whirled. "Not on me. I'm not sure where we put it."

Forbes nodded as if that was the answer he expected. "The first order of business is to find it. Now, given that we're more than likely trapped here for the night and the magic eater will track you to the station, we have limited choices."

"I want to hear them," Axel said.

Forbes poked the air. "The first choice is to run, but that doesn't always work. Erebus learns from his prey. He grows better, stronger. It's what makes him such a formidable opponent. The other choice we have is to trick him—but it'll only work once."

"Trick him?" Garrick asked. "How?"

Forbes licked his lips as if this choice was a delicious option. "We make Erebus think we don't have magic, that way he overlooks us. But like I said, this will only work once. After that, we've got to come up with a better plan."

Axel glared at Forbes. "How does it work, and why didn't you tell us any of this before?"

"Because I was recovering from the shock of meeting the magic eater, so I wasn't thinking clearly." He extended his palm. "Hand me the pin."

My gaze darted to Axel. Hand Forbes my family? If he was the man behind having us summon Erebus, then giving him the pin would be tantamount to handing my family over to a murderer.

He sensed Axel's hesitation. Forbes's fingers twitched. "It can work, but we have to be quick. The creature may show up any minute."

As if on cue, the glass in the windows shattered. I curled into a ball and slammed my eyes shut. Shards screamed past me. My arms burned as glass sliced into my flesh.

Under the cover of my hands I sneaked a glance at Axel to see him, eyes closed, place the pin in Forbes's palm. Forbes cupped the pin and chanted something.

Everything stopped. The world moved in slow motion, and I felt like we were suspended under water. I turned to look toward Erebus, but even that movement seemed to take an eon. Particles of glass blew around us, looking more like feathers than biting shards ready to scratch.

The tips of my ears tingled. My fingers felt charged as if an electric current was running through them. The odd sensation washed all the way to my toes.

I pivoted toward Axel. He slowly whipped toward Erebus, ready to fight.

Forbes cupped the pin in his hand, his head bowed.

The glass circled us like a tornado. It was a great cloud of debris that swirled and whirled. My gaze flickered to Garrick. He reached out as if about to shoot Erebus with a stream of magic.

The magic eater darted into the room. He seemed to suck up the glass or somehow the shards didn't touch him—I wasn't sure which was true, but he moved through the sea as if the shards didn't bother him.

Which they probably didn't, now that I thought about it.

Where I stood trapped in syrup that made me unable to move quickly, Erebus was a cheetah, floating between us, assessing each and every one of us.

I shivered as he approached me. If he attacked, I knew I wouldn't be able to fight back. This gooey magic that had me bound was too thick to move through.

His long face studied me. My heart jackhammered against my ribs, and I nearly choked under the creature's stare. His empty eyes and the dark hollow of a mouth were sickening up close.

His warm breath flowed over me, and I felt the strangest comfort before Erebus finally moved to Axel. Once the magic eater was finished with him, he darted to Forbes.

I don't know how long I held my breath, but it felt like an eternity as the creature sniffed up and down the old man. It seemed like Erebus knew Forbes was a person of interest, but he couldn't prove it.

Sweat trickled down my temples. Forbes's magic would either work or it would go very, very sour.

I would've crossed my fingers, but I couldn't move fast enough to do it. Finally, after what seemed like forever, Erebus drifted away from Forbes and darted to Garrick, studying him before whisking out the door.

Once Erebus was gone, it took a good five minutes before Forbes's spell wore off and I could move at a normal pace again.

First thing Garrick did was repair the windows. I glanced at the backs of my arms, which were lined with slices.

Axel crossed to me and curled his hands around my forearms. I flinched. "Ouch."

He didn't reply, only closed his eyes. A moment later my wounds healed. When he was done, Axel kissed my forehead.

"You okay?"

I nodded dumbly. "You?"

He grunted a reply that I took to mean *yes.*

Axel jerked his head toward Forbes. "Your plan worked. Let's hope it holds for the rest of the night."

Forbes grinned. He was obviously quite pleased with himself. "It'll hold. The magic eater won't be back—not tonight. We've managed to keep ourselves alive for one more day."

There was still something about Forbes that I didn't fully trust. "Why didn't you use that spell last night, when Erebus attacked you?"

"Because I was saving it," he snarled. "I couldn't exactly show my hand so early."

"But you used it tonight," I argued. "What's the difference?"

"Young lady," he said with distaste in his voice, "the difference is that we were stuck between a rock and a hard place. I had no other choice."

Forbes ran a hand over his silvery hair. "Now. If we're to survive and put Erebus back where he belongs, in that book, we've got work to do."

I scoffed. Was this old man delegating to me what to do? A man who other than this one spell, hadn't lifted a finger to help us?

Needless to say I was irritated.

I folded my arms. "Why should we listen to you?"

Forbes took his cane from the cell and moved to leave the station. He stopped at my question and slowly pivoted toward me. "Because if I hadn't been thrown in the pokey today, I could've helped y'all find a way to get Erebus back in his book. Plus, we could've done something even more important than that."

"Which is?" Axel said.

Forbes tsked. "You *younguns* don't know everything like you believe you do. Snow and Saltz are dead. Two incredibly talented magical people. If a magic eater can walk into a school and kill Saltz, then we have a real problem, and the problem isn't simply the magic eater."

"What is it?" Garrick asked.

"It's whoever tricked you into summoning Erebus in the first place. That's the person yanking the strings. Unless we can find them, we'll never get Erebus back in his book."

That made no sense to me. "Why not?"

"Because," Forbes snipped, obviously annoyed that he had to explain simple things to me, "whoever had Erebus summoned is probably blocking him from returning to the book. It's as simple as that."

He nodded toward the pin. "Now, I suggest you release Betty Craple and everyone else because we're going to need their help discovering who's actually behind this."

"Which means we go back to Snow's. To the day of the meeting."

Forbes smiled. A silver cap in his mouth glinted. "That's exactly right. We discover who sent Erebus and we can get rid of them. Otherwise..."

I cocked a brow. "Otherwise?"

Forbes sighed. "Otherwise we'll all die."

FIFTEEN

"Thank goodness someone finally got me out. I thought I'd be trapped in there forever, forced to listen to my mother and aunt argue about the best way to make blackberry cobbler."

Amelia sat in the living room, a blanket draped over her shoulders. She rocked back and forth. Obviously the strain of having been locked up with my family had gotten to her.

I patted her shoulder. "You'll be okay."

She shook her head. "You don't know what it was like. My mothers argued it wasn't their fault we got stuck in the pin, and Betty wanted to kill them. She almost magicked their mouths zipped shut."

I stifled a laugh.

Amelia suddenly shrieked. "I think I've got some sort of disorder now. I'm in shock."

I rubbed her head. "It's going to be okay." I pulled away from her and moved to stand by Axel, who had his back against the far wall and was facing the front door.

He wasn't going to let anything sneak up on him.

"Okay," Betty snapped. "Now that we're finally free, no thanks to my daughters"—she shot them a hard look—"we can figure out a plan moving forward."

Forbes took the wheel. "We need to go over the list of people who were at the meeting. Other than us, that is."

Betty thought for a moment. "It was most of the usual folks—no one stands out, but I have their names."

"Then we must talk to them—see if any seem suspicious," Forbes said. "See if any of them may have sent this plague down on us. We must split up."

Mint and Licky agreed to talk to some folks, as did CJ and Sylvia. Betty pinned her gaze on me.

"Pepper, Cordelia and Amelia, y'all need to head over to Snow's and see if there are any clues as to what happened."

Amelia scoffed. "We know what happened. We got tricked."

Betty glared at her. "But we need to know if there are any tidbits that could point to *who* did this. Remember, Snow was killed first."

I shot Cord and Amelia pointed looks. "Betty has a point."

"It's settled then. First thing in the morning, y'all will go over there."

"And I need the original spell," Forbes said. "The one y'all used to call the magic eater."

I glanced at Cordelia. "Do you have it?"

She shook her head. "I don't have it. Amelia does."

Amelia scoffed. "I don't have it, either. I thought Pepper had it."

Forbes ran a hand down his tired face. "I need to look at the original incantation. That's one way to figure out who summoned Erebus. Without it, this could take a long time."

My stomach soured. All eyes were on me. "Um," I finally mustered. "I'll search through my things."

"You'd better find it," Forbes snapped. "We must have that slip of paper."

"She'll find it," Betty said. "In the meantime I still want the girls at Snow's in the morning."

Betty continued to hand out assignments while Forbes nodded his head in agreement. When it was all finished, Axel leaned over and whispered in my ear.

"Be sure to take Hugo."

Fear spiked down my spine. If Axel wanted me to take the dragon, that meant he believed something bad would happen. "Why?"

Axel shrugged. "Just to be on the safe side. We've all got a lot to do. Just make sure you keep your dragon close."

"But before you said not to take him."

"I think it'll be okay, at least for right now. Erebus doesn't want you. But take Hugo, just to be safe."

Axel brushed the backs of his fingers down my arm. A sliver of desire shot straight to my gut. I cleared my throat to push those thoughts from my head.

"When I'm not with you," Axel continued, "Hugo is your best protection. Besides yourself, that is. He's your own personal bodyguard."

I smiled. "Will do."

~

THE SUN BURNED high and bright the next morning. As soon as pinks and blues cracked the horizon, I was up and ready to go. There was no work in Magnolia Cove right now. It seemed all hands were on deck to deal with the magic eater.

Even Snow and Saltz's funerals were on hold. Hopefully we'd have this whole situation resolved tonight and things would get back to normal.

I'd ripped apart my room searching for the original spell but hadn't been able to find out. Worry ate at me, and I spent the better part of the sunrise in the bathroom, dealing with an upset stomach.

By the time I was able to leave, I found Amelia and Cordelia sitting on my bed, impatience etched on their faces.

"I can't find it," I said. "Do you think a finding spell would help?"

"Let me focus," Cordelia said.

She closed her eyes. The room warmed with magic. The pressure continued until it popped.

"Something's blocking my attempt," Cordelia replied. She tossed herself on my covers and moaned. "How could we have lost it?"

I shook my head. "Don't feel bad. How were we supposed to know we'd need it to figure out who's behind this."

"There's no point in feeling sorry for ourselves," Amelia said tensely. "We need to go to Snow's." She hiked a shoulder. "Besides, maybe we'll find a clue there—something that will tell us exactly who did this."

I slipped into my shoes and pulled my hair into a ponytail. "Y'all ready?"

My cousins nodded. I snapped my fingers, and Hugo rose from his coiled position on the floor. "Come on, Hugo. Let's go."

We rode our cast-iron skillets to Snow's house. The place looked exactly as we had left it, door hanging from the frame. Dried leaves had blown inside the house, but Snow's body was gone, removed by the authorities.

Even with the sun shining brightly outside, only a fraction of that filtered inside. Dust motes floated on the few slices of sunlight that burst through the windows, but the house was still dark.

Amelia shivered. "This place gives me the creeps."

"Tell me about it." I brushed past her and headed toward the area where Snow had first offered me the paper. "We found the original spell beside Snow's body—the one I had given back to her. When she handed me the paper, I was standing here, beside this buffet."

Cordelia eyed the area. "Who else was nearby?"

I considered her question. "Satlz Swift and Sylvia were somewhat, but not right beside me. I think Forbes was on the other side of the room and CJ was milling about."

"Anyone else?" Amelia asked.

I thought about it, trying to remember who had been close at the time. "I spoke to Snow. She really grabbed my attention, telling me that I could clean up the same as Mint and Licky had. Then I handed the spell back to her and we left. It was that simple. There wasn't anyone else around. No one who could've known what we were talking about."

Then I remembered a strange bit of information, something that jarred my mind.

"What is it?" Cordelia said.

I grimaced. "Nothing. Just some silly notion I had."

"Nothing is too silly not to mention," Amelia prodded.

Hugo huffed in agreement.

I dragged my gaze to each of their faces and pointed to a silver box sitting atop a surface. "Snow told me that she'd trapped a mischievous spirit in that box. I wasn't sure if I believed her at the time, but what if… It's so stupid."

I raked my fingers down my face and exhaled a shot of air. "What if the creature in the box switched them?"

"But they're trapped," Amelia said. "I don't think that's possible."

"You're right. It was silly."

Cordelia clapped her hands. "Come on. Let's go find Snow's magic room. Pretty much every witch has one, and in it we might find clues as to what really happened."

It only took a few minutes to find said magic room. The room was white as, well, snow, and was in pristine condition—every vial dusted and every surface wiped of grime.

"Snow was definitely tidy," Amelia said.

While my cousins searched the room, I took the opportunity to peek at Snow's shelves. At least twenty leather-bound books, all with years printed on the spines, occupied an entire shelf by themselves.

"What are these?" I murmured. My fingers brushed the top of one dated *1999*. I slipped it out and peeled back the cover.

What have we done? The blight has taken over Magnolia Cove. What we thought was the right thing to do has backfired.

That was the first line, and it was handwritten.

"Snow's journal," I whispered.

I turned the page and kept reading. Turned out Snow was an excellent record keeper. She wrote about how the three witches and three wizards had worked to help the town but unleashed the blight, and then she wrote about how they had been able to stop the blight.

That was where *1999* ended. I was just about to pick up *2000* when Cordelia called me over.

Real solid information filled these books. One of these could hold the key to the answer we sought.

"Look at this, Pepper," she said.

I dragged myself away from the shelf and crossed to them. "What's up?"

Amelia stared in wonder at a silvery-looking solution in a mortar. She picked it up, and the substance remained congealed and unmoving.

I nodded toward it. "What's that?"

"Unless I'm wrong," Cordelia replied smartly, "that's Sticky Stuff."

"Okay," I said slowly, not understanding the importance. "You've got me. What's Sticky Stuff?"

"It's sticky," Amelia said.

Cordelia rolled her eyes. "We've already gone over that. Pepper wants to know what's important about it."

"Oh." Amelia clapped her hands. "Let's just show you. Cordelia, would you do the honors?"

Cordelia found a slip of paper sitting on a desk. She held it in front of her face while Amelia pinched off a bit of the Sticky Stuff.

"You ready?" Amelia said.

Cordelia nodded. "Just don't hit me in the eye."

"Well, don't put your eye where the paper is," Amelia retorted.

"I'm not trying to," Cordelia snapped. "But sometimes you have crappy aim."

"I do not have crappy aim!"

If these two continued to bicker, I'd never find out what the Sticky Stuff was. "Would you two stop and just show me? People's lives are on the line."

Amelia threw Cordelia a look full of contempt. "Hold the paper and don't move."

"Just go," Cordelia snapped.

Then in a flash, Amelia flicked the Sticky Stuff straight at Cordelia. A thin line of shimmery goo flew through the air and landed squarely in the center of the paper.

Amelia lightly flicked her wrist again, and the next thing I knew, the paper was sitting in Amelia's hand.

My cousin grinned proudly. "See? Isn't that cool?"

I rubbed away a worry line that had started forming between my eyes. "I guess so, but I don't see how it's relevant to us."

"It works backward too," Cordelia pointed out. "You can pull something toward you, or you can throw something at someone and make it stick, so to speak."

My cousins both eyed me victoriously, and it wasn't until that moment that I figured out what was going on. "Wow. You're saying that Snow made this and used it on me to give me the paper."

"Possibly," Amelia said. "But we found—"

A sound of bottles falling caught our attention. Amelia threw her hands into the air in fright, knocking over a beaker filled with a golden substance. She reached for it and, in the process, managed to knock over a vial filled with red powder.

"Oh no," she yelled. "Run!"

I didn't understand why I was supposed to run until glass shattered and the powders mixed.

A wall of flame shot up into the room, blocking me off from the bookcase.

Hugo howled at the fire. The dragon rose into the air, flapping his wings and screeching. I got the feeling he was trying to tell us we needed to leave.

"No," I screamed. "The journals!"

The one journal I wanted, the one that might tell us exactly who had tricked us into summoning the magic eater, now lay barricaded behind a wall of flame.

I reached for it, but Cordelia tugged my arm. "Don't, Pepper."

I flung out my arm. "Can't we put it out?"

Amelia shook her head. "It's powder flame. We can try, but it might make it worse."

"Try," I demanded.

Then the three of us sweet tea witches focused our magic. I

wanted the flames to die. I picked up the nearest thing I could find—a paperweight—and coaxed it into becoming water.

I threw the rock onto the fire. At the last second it transformed into a rod of water, splashing onto the flames. The fire hissed and sizzled, but it didn't sputter out.

"We have to call someone," I yelled. "Before the whole house goes up."

Cordelia's and Amelia's attempts to put the flames out didn't work. The heat increased.

"We have to go," Amelia shrieked.

I stared at the journals as they burned up, and I wanted to kick myself for not grabbing the one I needed. But I couldn't cry about it. I had to move on.

As we ran from the room toward the front of the house, I noticed something scurrying. I peered closer.

"Flower!"

The little possum scampered toward the front door. When she heard my voice, Flower turned.

"What happened to you?" I said. "We were worried."

Flower ran up to me. "Oh my gosh, Pepper. It was so dark that night I got lost and couldn't remember how to get back to the house."

"But you're a possum; you can see in the dark," I argued.

She patted her whiskers. "It had been a long time since I'd been in the forest."

"Come on," Amelia shouted. "The place is going to burn down."

I picked up Flower and tucked her under my arm. "Flower, we need your help. You might remember something from that day or know something about Snow that could help us find out who summoned the magic eater."

I rushed outside as Cordelia pulled out her phone to call the fire department. I realized I was sweating, so I settled Flower on the ground, pulled a tissue from my pocket and dabbed my skin.

"I'll help any way I can," Flower said. "But first there's something I have to tell you."

"Yeah, what is it?"

"When I got lost in the forest, I returned to that man's house."

"Forbes?"

"That's the one. I went back to his house and found something that might interest you."

"What's that?"

Flower's dark eyes looked glassy, as if she was about to cry. I felt that something really bothered her, almost frightened the creature.

I knelt and took her paws in my hands. "What is it, Flower? Whatever it is, you can tell me."

"I found something that makes me think the old man is the one who called the creature."

I had to admit with as much as Forbes had helped us lately, I didn't necessarily think he was guilty anymore. But if Flower had proof of Forbes being nefarious, I had to at least take a look at it.

"What did you find?" I asked.

"I found a list of names—the same names as the one the magic eater is going after. He's been marking them off, Pepper. Marking them off as if he's counting them one by one. But that's not the worst part. The worst thing was that his name wasn't on the list—not at all."

I nibbled my bottom lip. "Which means Forbes doesn't plan on dying."

Flower nodded. "That's what I think, too. He wants everyone else dead but not himself." She yanked my shirtsleeve. "If you don't believe it, come and see for yourself."

I shook my head. "That won't be necessary. I believe it."

I ground my teeth. Now all I had to do was prove it.

SIXTEEN

*W*e waited until the fire department arrived before leaving. With this new information that Flower had given me, I knew we had to get to the house and tell Betty.

She'd have an idea of how to get the truth out of Forbes.

We sailed through the sky on our cast-iron skillets. The sun was already high in the clouds. This day was burning away faster than I liked.

My stomach seized, and the panic of seeing the magic eater gnawed at me. I'd probably have an ulcer the size of Canada by the time this was over.

I glanced at Cordelia, who I knew was really taking the brunt of this. Her mouth was set in a determined line. I had the feeling that not only was Cordelia berating herself, she was still convinced she needed to hand herself over to Garrick when this was all over.

I think all three of us did. We were negligent with magic and should never have worked a spell that we didn't know one hundred percent came from a decent source. Yes, we'd seen Licky and Mint work it, but the words had been wrong.

Wrong. All of them.

"Do any of y'all remember the spell?" I yelled above the wind screaming in my ears.

"A little," Amelia said.

"Not much," Cordelia admitted.

"Since we can't find it, we need to try to put the words back together, see if we can come up with the original. Otherwise we'll never be able to get rid of Erebus."

Cordelia nodded. "As soon as we land."

As we flew over Bubbling Cauldron, I noticed a huge gathering in the park.

I pointed. "What's that?"

Amelia peered down. "I see Betty surrounded by a whole bunch of folks."

Cordelia shook her head. "Who wants to guess Betty has a plan?"

I would've laughed if the situation hadn't been so serious. "I say we go down and find out what it is."

We landed. I gently lowered Flower onto the soft grass. People milled about, congregating toward Betty.

"Get your magic eater protection right here, folks. Magic eater protection!"

The sound of Betty's voice made the tiny ulcer that gnawed at my stomach grow even worse. What was my grandmother doing?

"Don't be shy, y'all," Betty yelled. "You need magic eater protection—I've got magic eater protection. Guaranteed to work."

Bodies jam-packed the park. Flower huddled at my feet while Hugo sailed through the air, diving and rolling playfully.

I only wished I could've felt so confident that everything would be okay.

"Step right up, folks," Betty continued to say.

"Should we wait in line?" Amelia said. "We need magic eater protection."

Cordelia rolled her eyes. "Come on. Let's see what this is about."

We reached Betty, who stood with CJ and Sylvia, passing out cups full of magic eater protection. Betty spotted us and smiled widely.

"Girls, thank goodness you're here." She shoved a full cup in my hands. "Pass this to whoever wants it."

"What's this all about?" I whispered harshly. "We know there's no such thing as magic eater protection."

Betty just smiled and nodded. "Got to keep the people protected."

I was tempted to grab my grandmother by the collar and take her around back for a good talking-to.

Just then CJ smiled at me. "Pepper, how about some magic eater protection?"

I sidled up next to him and lowered my voice. "Just what's going on here?"

"Golly gee, Miss Dunn, what makes you think something's going on?"

I shot him a scorching look. "Come on, CJ."

"Well"— his voice dropped to a whisper—"to tell you the truth, Miss Dunn, your grandmother has made a truth serum."

My eyelids flared. "And she's giving it to the entire town?"

CJ nodded proudly. "Yep. Then she's gonna find out who's responsible for this mess."

I raked my fingers down my face. Of all the harebrained ideas— drugging the town to find out the truth wasn't only insane, it was also probably not exactly legal.

"What's going on here?"

Speaking of the devil, Garrick Young strode up, a posse of officers behind him. His dark eyes moved from the cauldron full of liquid to the growing crowd. His lips were drawn into a tight line that did not look to break into a smile anytime soon.

"What's this about magic eater protection?" he said.

Without missing a beat Betty handed him a cup. "Would you like some?"

Garrick scowled. "No, I would not. I would like you to cease and desist handing this out to folks."

Betty gave a cup to a witch that looked eager for the remedy and crossed to Garrick, pushing folks out of her way with her ample bosom.

"Listen here, Garrick. This is important business."

"You and I both know such a potion doesn't exist," he argued.

"Shhh," she said. "You'll tell everyone!"

I shook my head and moved to them. "It's a truth serum, Garrick."

Garrick shook his head and stared at the sky. He pointed an accusatory finger at me. "Are you responsible for letting her do this?"

I shook my head. "No! Of course not. I just found out."

"It's to find out who's behind this," Betty admitted. "I've handed out serum to half the town."

"And that'll be quite enough." Garrick crossed to the cauldron and picked it up. "No one else will be getting any more of this serum. Betty Craple and company are officially out of business."

The crowd crowed in exasperation. Garrick shook his head. "I'm sorry but this is it. Y'all can't have any more."

"That's okay," Betty shouted. "Because whoever gave my daughter the spell for the magic eater can step forward now."

All I heard was the sound of cicadas in the trees. To me it was akin to crickets chirping.

"Tell me now if you're the one who gave her the spell," Betty said again.

Still more cicadas.

"Well dagnabbit, I gave that potion to just about every person in this town," Betty grumbled. "Who the heck is behind the magic eater?"

I shot her a hard look. "I think it was Snow and Forbes."

Betty cocked a brow. "You got proof?"

I nodded. "Come on. Let's get back to the house."

Betty, my cousins and I, along with Hugo and Flower, headed back to the house. CJ and Sylvia promised to come by later, closer to dark.

When we arrived, I steered Betty to the dining room table and sat her down.

"I'll make lunch," Cordelia said.

"No, you won't," I said. "I'll do it. I need time to think."

Cordelia looked surprised that I would snap at her, but she did as I commanded.

I made a quick meal of chicken salad sandwiches and chips and brought it out for my family.

I settled the tray down and exhaled deeply. "We set Snow's house on fire."

Betty's eyes widened. "You did what?"

"Yep," Amelia chirped. "But it was an accident."

Betty dropped her face into her hands. "Now we have nothing to go on."

"That isn't true." I sat and plated sandwiches and a handful of chips for each of us. "We found Sticky Stuff."

Amelia nodded enthusiastically. "Which means that Snow could've thrown the spell onto Pepper herself."

I nodded toward Flower, who sat at my feet, her large eyes begging for scraps. I handed her a wedge of sandwich. "And Flower said that in Forbes's house there's a list with everyone's name. Snow and Saltz were already marked off. Forbes's name wasn't on it."

"I say we torture it out of him," Betty said. "Put a feather to his feet. Make him laugh. That man hates to laugh. We get him to do that and he just might spill the beans."

"But he wants us to find the spell," Cordelia argued. She paused. "How did it go?"

I racked my brain. "Sprite of blight—was that it?"

"Yes," Cordelia exclaimed. "That's how it started. I'll be darned if I don't stop this thing."

Betty shot her a confused look. "You?"

"Yes." Cordelia stared at the table as dots of pink flared on her cheeks. "This whole thing is my fault. I demanded Amelia get rid of those mason jars because I had a date with Garrick. I'm the one who forced Pepper and Amelia to work the spell. If it hadn't been for me, none of this would've happened."

Betty shook her head. "I told Amelia I wanted the jars gone, too. Amelia, where are the jars?"

My cousin finished crunching a chip. "I got Erasmus to magic most of them away, given the situation. I still have a few I'm holding onto to clean."

Betty rubbed her chin. "For all I know someone had been planning this for years and only waiting until now for the time to be right. We're all old—well, I'm old and so is Forbes. Someone's final revenge on us for things we did when we were stupid. I would say young, but I wasn't young at the time, either."

Amelia blew out a shot of air. "Betty, I don't think you were ever young."

Betty scowled at her before turning her attention back to Cordelia. She squeezed Cordelia's arm. "You are not to blame."

My cousin clasped a hand over Betty's. "But I am. It's nice of you to try to be my grandmother and save me, but there's no saving this. I'm impatient, snarky and just plain rude sometimes. If I hadn't been so selfish, I wouldn't have called the magic eater here to begin with. Pepper didn't want to work the spell."

Cordelia's gaze flickered to each of us in turn. "I'm sorry."

"We will make this right," I said.

"How?" Cordelia said. "It's because of me that two people are dead. *Two*. I can't forgive myself for that."

My gaze darted from Cordelia to Amelia, whose neck was flushed a deep shade of red, to Betty, whose lips were in a taut line.

They were thinking exactly what I was—how could Cordelia make it up? How was it possible to bring back people from the dead?

"You didn't kill them," Betty said. "Erebus did. Erebus sucked them dry. Not because of you but because of someone else." She paused to make sure her words sank in. "Now. Let's return to the spell. What were the words?"

"Sprite of blight," I whispered. "Sprite of sprite?"

Cordelia nodded. "Something like that."

Betty frowned. "Are y'all sure?"

Suddenly Flower jumped onto the table. "Don't y'all think we should go to Forbes's house? Because I am super confident that he is absolutely guilty."

Betty flicked her hand toward the possum. "Maybe in a little bit. I'm trying to think."

She mumbled the words. So did I, and it was in that exact moment that a lightbulb went off in my head. I saw that the same thing happened to Betty.

"Sprite of blight," we said in unison.

"Oh my word," Betty said.

Flower stood on her hind legs and pointed with her little fingers. "Forbes is evil. I just know it. I feel it in my soul. We need to get him because he's the one involved."

I ignored the possum and spoke to Betty. "Are you thinking what I'm thinking?"

"What?" Amelia tugged on her soft curls. "Have y'all cracked the code or something?"

Cordelia leaned over the table. "If y'all have, you need to start telling us."

"That's the key," I said. "The word 'blight.'"

Betty snapped her fingers. "That's it. Why didn't we see it before?"

I rose. "Forbes was right."

"That scoundrel," Flower said. "He's the guilty one in all this."

"What's this all about?" Amelia said. "One of y'all needs to start talking now."

I exhaled a deep breath. "Forbes said whoever wanted the magic eater to surface, that their name would be in the spell."

Cordelia's jaw dropped. "Are you saying—"

"We really should get to Forbes's house," Flower insisted. "In fact, I'm on my way there now."

We ignored her. "It's the blight!" Amelia gasped. "But how?"

"The blight would have to have physically manifested itself," Betty said. "That's the only way."

"And the one being we've constantly encountered, who was trapped by Snow from the very beginning is—"

Amelia sucked air. "Flower!"

All eyes turned to the possum. Flower's eyes widened. She shook her head. "What are y'all saying?"

It all made sense. Flower had insisted that Snow had locked her up under the house. Flower had said she sometimes sneaked inside. She could have slipped me the spell with the Sticky Stuff. Plus, the one biggest thing about the whole mess was that neither my grandmother nor any other of the five had seen Snow get rid of the blight.

They'd never watched it.

It all made perfect sense. Flower was the physical manifestation of the blight. She had orchestrated every piece of this, creating chaos and staying with us. Why? To make sure everyone suffered from her revenge?

I rose, fists clenched, ready for a fight—with a possum, of all things. "Flower, you are Blight. You've caused this entire scenario. You are responsible for Snow's and Saltz's deaths. Stay where you are!"

I leaped toward her, but she scampered for the front door. Amelia darted toward the possum, cutting her off from escaping.

Flower turned and scurried toward the kitchen.

"Cordelia," I shouted.

My cousin extended her hand, and a line of magic zipped across the room, aimed directly at the possum.

Flower, seeing the magic heading toward her, twisted her front legs, trying to grab the hardwoods to break her run. She dug her claws into the floor and skidded across the smooth wood.

Cordelia's magic hit the base of the door just as Flower stopped.

I leaped over a dining room chair, hell-bent on catching the rodent.

But Flower had time to tuck and run, which is what she did—readjusting her trajectory. She scampered under the dining room table and chairs.

"I'll get you," Betty yelled.

My grandmother swatted at the creature, but Flower dodged her grasp. The possum shot out from the table and headed up the stairs.

"I'm on it," Amelia yelled.

She led the way up the stairs, taking them two at a time. The three of us reached the top and stopped.

Every bedroom door was open.

"Which way did she go?" I whispered.

Cordelia motioned for each of us to search our rooms. Betty

climbed up the steps slowly, and I motioned for her to check her own bedroom. She nodded and we split up.

Quiet filled my bedroom. Mattie lay by the window, and Hugo napped on my bed.

Some watch-animals they were. They didn't even wake up from all the commotion downstairs.

I padded softly across the floor. First place to check, under the bed. I leaned down and looked but no Flower.

I scanned the room's contents. Bookshelf—empty except for books. Dressing table? Drawers closed. Desk? Cluttered with books. Bed? The foot lay covered in clothes that I really needed to put away or toss in the hamper.

The bed. That's where she had to be. That little sucker was hiding under the clothes.

Okay. How was I supposed to do this? I walked to my dresser and opened the drawer that held all my T-shirts. Y'all, I had a lot of T-shirts. I mean, they were just one of those clothing items I tended to collect. Go to the fair—buy a T-shirt to remember it. Take a vacation —oh, had to buy a T-shirt. I mean seriously, lots of T-shirt buying went on in my life.

I nabbed one and stalked quietly back over to the mound of clothes.

After staring at it for a good ten seconds, I figured out which pile she was hiding under. That little critter was tucked under a pair of brown shorts. All I had to do was pick up the shorts and throw the T-shirt on top and I had her.

Easy as pie.

My heart raced as I stared at the pile. Had to get this right. If I nabbed Flower, then we were golden. We could get her to call off the magic eater. It could be done.

My breath hitched, and I forced it to smooth out. From shooting mistletoe out of trees when I was a kid, I knew the best time to fire was after an exhale.

That's how I would approach this now.

I inhaled deeply, let it slowly seep from my body and moved.

AMY BOYLES

I fisted the shorts from the bed, expecting to see Flower underneath it. The possum was nowhere to be found.

Maybe she was in someone else's room. Maybe she wasn't in my bedroom at all.

I peeked my head out of the door and saw Amelia and Cordelia both standing there. They shrugged.

None of us could find her.

Betty stepped out of her bedroom and motioned for us to meet in the hall.

She dropped her voice to a whisper. "She's hiding good. If we want to find this critter, we'll have to do this the hard way."

I twisted the ends of my hair into a knot at the base of my neck. "What do you mean?"

"We have to screw with her psychologically." Betty's gaze darted to each of us. "We'll have to trick her into thinking we're gone. Make her think we believe she's outside, and we'll pretend to go out the door."

Amelia frowned. "Can she hear you right now?"

Betty shook her head. "Kid, I've been at this living thing a long time. I spelled us so that we're in a conversation bubble."

"What's that?" I asked.

Cordelia answered. "It's where only we can hear each other."

"Okay, good," Amelia said. "Because if Flower hears us, then the whole gig is up."

"Like I was saying," Betty started up again, "we pretend to go outside and wait. She'll come down to check. When she does..."

"We nab her," I said.

Betty nodded. "We nab her."

"Okay," I said loudly. "We can't find the possum."

"We're still in the conversation bubble," Betty pointed out. "She can't hear you."

I scoffed in frustration. "Can you please let us out?"

My grandmother tapped her nose. A tendril of magic uncoiled from her nostril and swirled around us. It looped around our heads and disappeared.

"Well," Betty said loudly, "looks like that Flower got outside. What say the four of us go out to check?"

"Sounds good," Amelia said. "You don't think she hurt herself climbing out a window, do you?"

The three of us shot her harsh looks. I'm pretty sure we were all thinking the same thing—we didn't care whether or not the creature had hurt herself because she's the one who caused this whole mess.

"Nah." Cordelia waved her hand. "That little girl is too light to have hurt herself."

"She's also nimble," Betty said.

"Yeah," I added. "Everyone knows possums are as nimble as they get."

"Right," Amelia said, suddenly looking confused. Not sure why, but that was the expression on her face. Her brows were stitched together, and her lips puckered up in question. "Okay. Well, let's go outside and check."

We stomped so hard going down the stairs that the walls shook.

"Discreet much?" Cordelia murmured.

"We're not supposed to be," Amelia whispered.

"I know," Cordelia snapped. "That's the point."

"Oh."

Betty pointed to the front door. "Pepper and I will go out that way. The two of y'all head out back."

"Okay," Cordelia shouted.

They tromped toward the kitchen door and stopped in front of it. Betty opened the front door and slammed it shut—twice.

Then we waited.

The clock on the wall seemed to tick into infinity before we finally heard the first stirring of movement.

Betty and I had prime viewing toward the top of the stairs. As soon as a head poked out, I knew she'd be on it.

We would have to move quickly.

Something shuffled around slowly. Betty raised her hand, her magic ready.

Finally, a tiny nose peeked out from atop the stairs. It sniffed the air, and Flower's head came into view.

"Now," Betty shouted.

Blasts of magic spewed toward the creature. None of us wanted to hurt her. We only wanted to capture the rodent.

But Flower moved like the wind. She practically sailed down the steps.

Which, I'm going to be honest, completely freaked me out. Fight-or-flight took over my body, and I screamed as the white-faced creature headed toward me.

Fear fissured through me, but I had to capture her. I reached toward Flower as a blast of magic hit her squarely in the belly.

The possum was thrown to the ground. Suddenly we were all lunging toward her.

Magic blasted every which way, and I heard a crash, as if a window had shattered.

There was no time to look. I dived toward Flower, colliding with Amelia. Our heads knocked together. I ignored the pain shooting down my neck, but I couldn't ignore the fog that took over my brain. I shook it off and snatched at the possum, but she scampered up my arm and over my body.

"I've got her," Betty shouted.

My grandmother, God bless her soul, shot a wave of magic that missed the scampering critter. Betty's mouth set into a determined line, and she flung herself at Flower.

I don't know how she did it, how Betty's sixty-something-year-old body managed to sail through the air. She landed on the floor, and Flower took the opportunity to climb up Betty's rump.

My gaze locked on what lay behind Flower—the shattered window. The possum turned around, shot me a look full of victory and made a flying leap toward the window.

"Stop her," I yelled.

Cordelia sprang from across the room, climbing over the couch and spraying a blanket of magic toward the window.

She was trying to seal it, I knew.

At the same time Flower jumped high. Her back legs kicked and her front paws paddled as if that would help her fly faster.

Cordelia's magic hit the window frame and started weaving a net from one side. It would thread all the way to the other, but would it stop Flower?

I held my breath and reached up, thinking I could lasso the rodent before she made it outside.

My magic hit Flower on the rump, propelling her through the window at the exact time that Cordelia's magical lace threaded in the center.

The lace closed the window, and I dashed to it in time to see Flower land safely on the other side.

She twisted her head around, shot me look of contempt and said, "See you later, sucker!"

With that Flower dashed off, darting down the street and out of sight.

I sighed in defeat, my shoulders slumping. I felt like we'd had the opportunity of a lifetime in our hands and it had been squandered, never to be seen again.

My face crumpled, and I raked my fingers down my face. "How? How will we ever find her now?"

Amelia reached for Betty, who swatted her away. "I'm not so old that I can't help myself, kid."

Betty righted herself with a bit of magic and smoothed her flowered dress. "Well, the blight got away. Time to regroup. We need a new plan."

Cordelia gave her an incredulous look. "Are you kidding? How're we going to find her now?"

Betty folded her arms and narrowed her eyes. "Where there's a will, there's a way, kids. Now round everybody up. It's going to be all hands on deck until we find that possum."

"How do you know she won't run off?" Amelia said.

Betty smirked. "That possum can't leave until all of us are dead. Until the magic eater finishes business, she'll be here and we'll find her—one way or another."

SEVENTEEN

"*B*ut how? How are we going to find Flower?"

After the fiasco at Betty's, I headed over to Axel's and explained the whole situation. Axel had spent the morning poring over old books with Forbes, trying to figure out a loophole that would send Erebus back.

Unfortunately for us, there wasn't a loophole.

And that didn't help the situation with Flower anyway. Even if we banished the magic eater to the book, the blight was still around.

Who's to say Flower wouldn't fool someone else into calling Erebus from his book?

Axel considered my question, tipping his head back and forth as he thought. "The first question we have to ask is not how to find Flower, but what is it she wants?"

"To get rid of everyone who summoned her to begin with?" I guessed. "What else could she want?"

Axel nodded slowly. "Right. So the blight was called here by six people; then the blight got trapped here. Does Flower think that by killing off the very people who summoned her, that she'll be able to leave?"

I shook my head. "Maybe there's more to it than that. Snow turned her into a possum. Maybe all Flower wants is to be turned back into herself."

Axel considered that. "It makes sense. Maybe there are clues at Snow's house."

I grimaced. "There might be if there's anything left."

Axel shot me a dark look. "What do you mean?"

I twisted my fingers. Boy, did I want to disappear. Like really wanted to disappear. "Well, um…"

"Pepper," Axel growled in warning. "What happened?"

"Cordelia, Amelia and I went to Snow's this morning. We were in her spell room, and some powders spilled, causing a fire. What stinks is that I found a whole slew of Snow's journals, but I don't know what was in them."

I balled my hands and pressed them into my eyes. "I don't know what's left of the house, and I tried to get the journals but the flames were too high."

Axel wrapped me into a hug. He threaded his fingers through my hair and sprinkled kisses down my cheek. He leaned back and pressed his lips to my right eye and then my left.

I couldn't help but smile at the feel of his lips on me.

"We might be able to summon the books back," he said, comforting me. "We'll go to Snow's and see."

I sniffled and knuckled a bit of moisture from the bottom of my eye. "Okay. There may be clues left."

Axel kissed my forehead. "Come on. Let's load up in the truck and head over."

Snow's house still smoked when we arrived. It looked like a skeleton, all charred bones and steaming chimney. A few firefighters worked magic with water to calm what remained of the smoking embers.

"This looks so bad," I murmured. "Do you think we'll be able to find anything?"

Axel winked at me. "I don't know. Let's go look."

I got out, and Axel came around, threading his fingers through mine. "Thanks for not guilting me about this."

Axel shook his head. "Are you kidding? There are so many crazy things in play here. The first was Snow; then your aunts have caused a ruckus. It's all going to work out. You just need to have faith."

I nodded. Faith was harder to come by right now than he could imagine. As much as I wanted to think about how things had spiraled out of control, the best thing I could do for myself and my family was to follow Axel through the rubble and see if there was a way to bring back those journals.

"Where were they?"

I pointed to a far corner of the house. "Over there."

We picked our way through the wet and sloshy mess. I barely recognized the table my cousins and I had found the Sticky Stuff on. It looked like a heaping mess of charred wood and ash.

I nodded toward where the bookcase had been. "That's where the journals were."

Axel dropped my hand and planted himself in front of the smoking wall. The paneling was burned away. Part of the bookcase remained and amazingly enough, a few of the journals were still there, though they were little more than heaps of black paper.

"I don't know which was the exact journal, but it was one of these."

"Stand back," Axel commanded.

I retreated a step and watched as Axel flung out his arms. Magic swirled around his hands, circles and squares appearing out of thin air beside his elongated fingers.

His forearms tensed and Axel chanted low. It was like my fiancé was calling on the powers of the universe to help him with his magic.

A gust of air swooshed past, picking the hair off my neck. A shiver raced down my back, and I hugged my arms around me. Axel's chanting increased. The air buzzed with electricity. The humidity thickened and the atmosphere seemed to gain weight, pushing down on me.

As the intensity grew, the wind picked up, blowing Axel's hair something fierce.

He yelled something I couldn't hear, and then it felt like the air contracted, buoying out.

The next thing I knew the journals had returned. They were still a little charred, but they were back—both shelves of them.

"Oh my gosh." I moved past Axel and ran a finger down the binding of the one marked *2000*. "How did you do that?"

Axel shrugged. "Just a little extra magic I've been holding on to."

I gave him a skeptical look. "Little bit of magic, my rear end. That was almost a tsunami of power."

Axel nodded to the books. I swear pink dotted his cheeks. "Is the one you need here?"

I dragged my gaze from him and slid a volume from the case. "It is." A well of happiness sprung up within me. I threw my arms around Axel and kissed his cheek. "You're a life saver. Seriously. Thank you."

Axel's lips grazed mine. "You're very welcome," he murmured. Our gazes locked, and heat surged down my body. His blue eyes speared my heart to my spine. Every cell in my body buzzed with the electricity that coiled between us.

"What else are fiancé's for?" he said coyly.

"This is what you're for. Oh, that and making me extremely happy, of course."

He laughed. "Of course. Come on. We don't have a lot of time."

I grabbed another volume, just in case we needed it to answer other questions—the one dated *1999*.

"Let's look around a little bit," Axel said. "See if there are any clues under the house that may help us figure something out about Flower."

He led the way, and I cracked the spine of one of the journals. I scanned the pages, looking for anything that had to do with the blight.

Finally I found an entry. "Snow wrote that when she tried to send the blight back, it wouldn't go. The thing was a mass of energy, a huge ball that couldn't be contained and couldn't be destroyed."

We reached the edge of the crawl space, and Axel started sifting through the ash.

"So she put the blight in a possum's body, or turned the blight into the possum," Axel said.

"And never told anyone." I shook my head. "If only Snow had told someone what she had done, maybe this could've been avoided."

127

Axel raked his fingers through the dirt. "You're talking about a woman who caught creatures. Snow thought she could do anything. Thought she was capable of it all."

I nodded. "The possum got the last word. I wonder how long Flower had been planning this?"

"Probably from the moment Snow trapped her." Axel found a stone and palmed it. "Is there anything else in there? Anything that gives us a clue how to send her back?"

"From what Snow wrote, it appears that the blight simply didn't want to go."

"But why wouldn't Snow tell anyone?" Axel mused. "She told the others she would deal with it. That she could handle it."

"Pride?" I said.

Axel glanced up from the dirt. "Have you ever been so prideful that if you made a horrible mistake, you wouldn't tell anyone?"

I cringed. "No, even I don't have that much pride. If I do something wrong, especially something dangerous, then I let someone know."

"Exactly," Axel said. "So that doesn't sit with me. Just because Snow couldn't send it back, it doesn't add up that she wouldn't tell someone. Just think about it—if you'd released a blight and then couldn't deal with it, wouldn't you be afraid that it would return? You'd want to make sure it could be controlled. Otherwise the consequences would be disastrous."

I stared at the dirt Axel was sifting as his words seeped into my brain. "So if she told someone, then you think that someone else helped her and knew all about Flower."

Axel continued to search the dirt.

"What are you looking for, exactly?"

"Something that proves I'm right."

"And you think you're going to find it in there?"

He clicked his tongue. "Tell you what—you search the book while I do this, and we'll see who comes up with the answer first."

"You're on."

As much as it would have seemed this was a game, it wasn't. Axel

dragged the dirt while I searched for any clue that someone in the six
—someone else knew about the blight and her alter ego Flower.

If we could figure out who else knew about her, then it was likely
that other person may have an idea how to catch her. If we caught her,
then we could get Flower to call off the magic eater—or at least use
our magic to figure out a way to deal with the Erebus as long as we
had Flower.

It was worth a shot. I peeled back page after page, sifting through
Snow's writings as Axel sifted the dirt. I'd already uncovered where
Snow couldn't find a way to send the blight back.

"Aha," I said. "You're right."

"Did you question it?" Axel said sarcastically.

I shoved his knee with my toe. "No. Of course not." My finger slid
over the words. "Here Snow mentions reaching out to someone, but
she doesn't mention who."

"It's got to be in there," Axel replied.

I scanned more text. There were hints that there was another
person, but nothing about who. Snow explained that she had needed
another to offer guidance on what she should do. Snow already knew
that she couldn't banish the blight, but what to do with it?

Snow would need a vessel, something with hard lines and edges to
hold the blight. Something concrete—which was when Snow had the
idea to put the blight in an animal.

Which meant that Flower wasn't purely blight. Flower had been a
living, breathing possum, only she'd been imbued with the essence of
the blight.

Flower had been a living breathing possum…

I gasped. My lungs clutched for air. "Axel."

"Found something else?"

"I think Flower was a familiar."

He frowned. "Snow's?"

I shook my head. "No. Someone else's. Snow realized she needed a
body to put the blight in. Obviously she couldn't use a human, so she
stuck it in a familiar."

He smirked. "And she wouldn't use her own."

I nodded. The slow workings of the realization sank into me. "And if she had to reach out to someone and let them know what had happened and told them she needed a familiar, one of the six would've been the easiest to convince."

Axel closed his eyes. "The easiest witch or wizard to get a familiar out of would also have been the most innocent."

"CJ Hix," we said in unison.

I flipped pages, madly searching for the name. "It makes the most sense. Snow would've reached out to CJ, knowing he'd never say anything because he was so young. She would've asked for his familiar, and CJ would've handed her over. Snow would've then put the blight in Flower's body and locked her away under the crawl space."

I frowned. "But why didn't anyone ever suspect there was something strange about Flower?"

Axel raked his thumb over his jaw. "I think Snow kept her hidden. Maybe as she got older she didn't mind if Flower was seen by people, but at first it would've looked too suspicious."

I nibbled the inside of my mouth, trying to think. "But what about your idea that Snow would've needed guidance?"

Axel shook his head. "She wasn't getting any from CJ Hix. Not at his age."

"Do you think he even remembers any of it?" I folded my arms. "He never mentioned that Flower was his familiar."

Axel chuckled bitterly. "I'm sure he remembers." Fire lit in Axel's eyes. "We just need to find out how much."

EIGHTEEN

CJ Hix was at home, readying for the coming night. When CJ answered his door, the man was decked out in all kinds of talismans and magical objects.

"Wards," he explained, leading us inside. "I'm not risking the magic eater getting me. I lot of it's stuff I've collected over the years."

CJ raised a big golden disk that hung around his neck. "Can I interest you in something, Miss Dunn?"

I shook my head. "No thanks. Axel and I are here because we discovered something very interesting."

CJ yanked a silver chain. "Good and tight," he said, satisfied. "Now." The realtor shot us a lopsided grin. "What did y'all find that was so interesting?"

"Did you ever give your familiar to Snow?" Axel asked.

CJ jutted out his chin in thought. "Well, let me think about that." He tapped a finger to his temple. "As a matter of fact, I sure did. A possum."

I closed my eyes. "That possum became Flower. Snow used her to hold the blight."

CJ's eyes widened. "You don't say?"

Axel's jaw clenched. "We do say. CJ, we need your help."

"Anything."

"What can you remember about what Snow needed?"

CJ scratched his chin. "She said she needed my familiar, so I let her have it. I didn't know for what, and to be honest, it was so long ago I forgot all about it. But you say Flower was my familiar? Golly gee, I just never would've guessed that. But her name wasn't Flower back then. When she was my familiar her name was Cutie."

CJ frowned. "But did she recognize me? Does she know who I am?"

Axel scratched his cheek. "It's possible the blight has more control than Cutie. Whatever her name, we need to find her," Axel said. "She's missing. If we don't catch Flower, we won't be able to put this whole magic eater issue to rest. If we can catch her, we can stop this—stop everything."

CJ's lips formed a thin line. "When she was my familiar, we would often go into the Cobweb Forest."

"Of course," I murmured sarcastically. "You couldn't go somewhere easy like the beach."

"Oh no, Miss Dunn," CJ said good-naturedly. "You know there are no beaches around here. But there are good hiding spots in the Cobweb Forest—if you don't want to be found."

"And I take it you didn't," Axel said.

CJ nodded. "It wasn't always easy growing up. There was lots of yelling in my house. Lots of anger, but there were places I could go and feel safe."

"In the forest of all places," I murmured.

"Right."

Axel's blue eyes turned steely with determination. "Assuming the blight holds on to any of the memories from when Flower was Flower, where were the places you used to haunt?"

CJ stroked his chin. "Let me think. There were three main places we used to go. The first was under the Blustery Bluffs. The second was down by the big tree—the big oak."

"I know it," I said.

Axel nodded. "Me too."

"And the third," CJ continued, "was at Crossing Creek."

"I get why Blustery Bluffs are called that—they're windy, right?" I said. "But I don't understand the Crossing Creek."

Axel frowned. "It's said with the right magic and at the right time of year you can cross into a different time."

I frowned in appreciation. "Is that true?"

CJ shrugged. "Never happened when I was there, but I never knew the magic that would do such a thing."

My gaze locked with Axel's. "So those are our options?"

"It's the best plan we've got. Find Flower and make the blight stop the magic eater."

"How long until sunset?" I said.

CJ glanced out the window. "Another two or three hours."

Axel pressed his hand to the small of my back. The gesture gave me some comfort because the night ahead might be our most trying.

Axel's words nearly came out a growl. "Then let's get a game plan."

The game plan turned out to be simple. We would split up to search for Flower. Some folks would stay around places where we knew Flower had shown up before—Snow's and even our house.

We knew for a fact that the blight would want to make sure that Erebus did his job. To see that to the finish, that meant Flower might stay near other homes, including Forbes's and Sylvia's, so folks also remained camped out there—but not Forbes or Sylvia because there was no reason to make them sitting ducks.

Which meant many of us were heading into the Cobweb Forest to hopefully find a possum in a haystack.

"If anyone finds Flower," Betty said later, "then you contact Sylvia, CJ, Forbes and me immediately. The four of us will be together, waiting."

A dozen people stood crammed inside Betty's living room including Axel, what was left of the six, my cousins, aunts, and several police officers.

"I'll be with them," Axel said.

"So will I," Garrick added. "They'll be protected, but we have to find the possum."

"What about a plan for Erebus," I said. "It seems risky to keep everyone together."

Betty shot Forbes a knowing look. "We have a plan."

"One the rest of us can't know," I said.

She nodded. "For our safety. We don't know what sort of connection Flower may have with Erebus. If they can communicate and someone mentions details to Flower, the magic eater may well discover things we don't want him to."

"We don't have much light left," I said. "We'd better leave."

Betty nodded; her lips were tight in a line of worry. "Here are your assignments."

Amelia, Cordelia and I were sent to Blustery Bluffs. Of course we were. It figured I'd be sent to the one place I wasn't particularly crazy about—the Cobweb Forest.

"Anyone got a map?" I said.

"I do." Cordelia pulled a well-worn paper map from her backpack. "The Blustery Bluffs shouldn't be too far away. I don't think it'll take us any longer than ten minutes from this trail."

We stood at the mouth of the forest. A trail lay like a tongue in front of us, the mouth formed by bent willows. The light receded as the trail forked.

I shook off a shiver that raced down my spine. "Let's get this over with."

"I hope Flower shows up someplace soon." Amelia tugged at her wispy-stranded hair. "I just want this over with."

"I know." Cordelia set off down the path. "Let's just hope the Blustery Bluffs aren't as bad as they used to be."

That did not sound good. "What do you mean?"

"Last time we were here, Cordelia and I just about got blown off the bluffs," Amelia explained.

"So they're pretty windy," I said, already hating this assignment.

Amelia nodded knowingly. "Definitely."

I tucked in my shirt and readied for the bluffs.

"Doesn't something about this whole thing seem strange to you," I said.

"All of it does, actually," Cordelia said.

"Why would Flower need us to recite the incantation?" I asked. "Why couldn't she just do it herself? Why have we been dragged into this whole thing to begin with?"

Cordelia thought about it for a moment. "Maybe it has to do with the sort of magic that the blight possessed. Maybe you have to be human to summon from the book."

Amelia pulled a bag of nuts from her backpack and popped a few in her mouth. "I bet that's it. It makes sense that the incantation can only be worked by someone who's human."

"Yet they need Flower to call off Erebus," I pointed out.

"Everything we've tried hasn't worked. We got him back into the book but he jumped back out but now we'll use Flower to capture him? How?"

Amelia took this one. "Maybe Flower can be coerced into calling off Erebus?"

Cordelia shook her head. "No. If they can send the blight back to where she came from, she'll vanish and Erebus will disappear. It's as simple as that."

"But if Snow couldn't figure out a way to send the blight back, what makes us think we can?" I pointed out.

"Have you thought that maybe Snow didn't try?" Amelia said.

I grimaced. "That's not the sense I got. Not from her journal. In her journal it seemed like Snow tried to send it back but couldn't."

Cordelia check her map and then continued walking. "Heck, maybe she asked Forbes for advice and he told her the wrong thing on purpose because he hated her."

I paused. "Do you think Forbes would do that?"

Cordelia shrugged. "I wouldn't put it past him. It's not as if Forbes is the most decent guy on the block."

"But what would he have to gain?" Amelia said.

"Ah, there's the real question," Cordelia posed. "What would Forbes have to gain by not telling Snow the truth?"

I shook my head. "There just wasn't anything in her journals about that."

Cordelia opened her palm, and a ball of light appeared there. "What if she didn't put it down for whatever reason?"

Amelia chewed on some invisible substance as she appeared to ponder that thought. "What if it's more than that? What if Forbes is responsible for the blight? Wouldn't that be crazy? What if Forbes is the one who wanted to call the blight down completely and now wants to cover his tracks?"

My feet stuck to the ground. "Are you kidding?"

Amelia hiked a shoulder. "I mean, it almost makes sense. Snow was way into capturing creatures. She wasn't stupid. How could she have called down a blight?"

"You think Forbes tricked her?" Cordelia said. "Tricked her, and then when she turned to him for help, he just dug the hole even deeper? Telling her to get CJ's familiar and lock the blight in that?"

I kept walking, crunching leaves under my feet. "It sounds stupid when you put it that way. I think we're way off. At best we can hope to capture Flower and see if that helps things."

Cordelia nodded. "I agree. Let's just take this one step at a time."

There was no way to prepare for the wind that ripped through the Blustery Bluffs. Blustery wasn't even a good word for it. It was horrible. By horrible, I don't mean ugly, I mean it was so windy I could barely see.

Wind screamed around me, slashing my hair against my cheeks. Cordelia pulled Amelia and me under a jutting rock.

"It's calmer in here."

The three of us huddled under the outcropping of rocks. "Why on earth would CJ ever come here?"

"I think it's kinda calming," Amelia said. "In a weird sort of way."

"Definitely weird," I said.

We sat under the boulders quietly, waiting for our chance to find and nab Flower. The wind howled, and I hugged my arms, trying to keep warm against the screaming blasts as they hurdled under the bluff.

"I don't think I'll ever come here again," I mumbled. "Even if Flower doesn't show up."

Cordelia nodded. "I totally agree. Not sure it's worth it here."

As darkness crept in, the wind died down to only a light scream. I could hear myself think again, and I prayed silently that Betty and everyone else remained safe.

A few minutes later Amelia nudged me. She pointed toward a bush. A spot of white could be seen behind it.

I narrowed my eyes at her. She nodded and pointed at both Cordelia and me, trying to communicate a plan.

Her plan looked like she wanted to go to KFC and eat a bucket of chicken.

Seriously, it was all bringing her hand to her mouth and then pointing it out toward the bushes.

I had no idea what she was saying. Cordelia's face held the exact same confused expression. I raised my palms and shrugged, which only made Amelia gesture even more furiously.

Cordelia looked exasperated as well until finally Amelia shouted, "All I'm saying is, let's go over there and get her!"

The sound of Amelia's voice made me cringe. At the same time, the spot of white shot up.

"Flower," I yelled.

This time we were ready. All three of us blasted our magic toward the possum. Don't worry, we had a plan. We weren't just throwing magic at her to harm the little critter.

Our magic encircled the possum, ballooning her in a ball. Flower shook with fright as we brought the ball back to us. I plucked it from the air and held the bubble, possum and all.

A slow smile of victory crept over my face. "Well, well, well. Nice to see you, Flower. We need some help."

NINETEEN

$\mathcal{W}$e scrambled away from the Blustery Bluffs as quickly as possible and got out onto an open trail in the forest.

"Should we let her out?" Amelia said.

"She has enough air," Cordelia said unsympathetically. "For everything she's put us through, that little rodent should have to suffer in a hot ball for a while."

Amelia nodded. "I was stuck in a pin for half a day."

I clicked my tongue. "That is true."

"Please," Flower said. "Let me out."

"No," I snapped. "Not until I take you to my grandmother and you promise to call off the magic eater."

Flower scratched at the ball. "I know y'all think I called the magic eater. I don't blame you."

"You are the blight," Amelia snapped. "We know who you are. Why else would you have run away?"

"I am the blight. That's true. But I used to be a familiar."

"We know all about that," I said coldly. "CJ told us that Snow had him hand over his familiar and that she then put you inside the possum's body."

"Please," Flower pleaded. "Just listen to me."

Amelia shone her flashlight on the trail. "It's not as if we have a choice not to. We're on our way back to the—"

"Don't say where we're headed," Cordelia snapped. "She might communicate with Erebus."

"I'm not communicating with the magic eater," Flower said proudly. "Why would I talk to him?"

"It's because of you that he was summoned." I squeezed the ball tightly, wanting to shake the possum. "Don't try to deny that you didn't."

Flower sat silently for a moment. "You're right. It was me that summoned the magic eater. It was all my fault. But I didn't do it because I wanted revenge."

Cordelia scoffed. "You didn't do it because you wanted revenge? What a bunch of baloney. Why'd you do it then? Just for kicks and giggles?"

"No, I didn't do it for that." Flower pressed her palm to the side of the bubble. "I did it because I was asked."

All three of us stopped, our feet sticking to the forest floor. I spoke first, slowly and deliberately. "What do you mean, you were asked?"

Flower cleared her tiny throat. "I meant I was asked to slip you the paper. I was told that I would finally be free from the crawl space."

I exchanged a charged look with my cousins. "You were asked to slip me the paper?"

Flower nodded. "Yes. I can get up into the house. I could until it burned down, so I gave it to you."

Cordelia yanked the ball from me and brought the possum to eye level. "Who told you all that?"

Flower paused. When she didn't answer, Cordelia pushed the bubble back into my arms. "She's lying. The possum is only telling us that so we'll be confused. So that the magic eater can have his way and hurt our family. She's not helping. The possum is only trying to hurt us."

"No, it is true," Flower protested. "I was given the spell and the Sticky Stuff. I put it in your pocket, Pepper, when you left. After you

139

spoke to me. When you turned around, I slipped it into your pocket. I gave you the spell that started this whole thing."

"For your revenge," Cordelia said bitterly. "We know all you wanted was your revenge that you couldn't be sent back to whatever hole you were summoned from. We all know this."

Cordelia flung her arms out. "Why are we even standing here listening to this?"

"Because she might be telling the truth," Amelia said quietly. "Everything she says may help us send Erebus back." Amelia gently took Flower from my arms. My cousin studied the possum and in a soothing voice said, "Flower, can you please tell us who gave you the piece of paper? Can you tell us that?"

Flower smoothed her whiskers. "It puts everyone at risk."

"Everyone's already at risk," I argued.

"She means herself," Cordelia said. "That's who she's worried about."

Flower nodded. "If I said anything, I was told I'd be destroyed."

"And being stuck in the body of a rodent is so much better," Cordelia mumbled.

Annoyed that my cousin was being so immature, I whirled on her. "Will you quit? She's trying to help us."

"No," Cordelia spat. "All she's trying to do is save herself. She doesn't want to help. If she had, the creature would've done that days ago."

Cordelia's words struck deep. I stared at Flower, at her deep black eyes and at her tiny nose and delicate face. Everything Cordelia said was true, but what if more was going on? More than any of us had anticipated or even considered?

"So," Cordelia said tersely, "instead of telling us the information, you were afraid of being destroyed—when you knew all along that people were being picked off one by one."

"She's trying to help us now," Amelia pointed out. "If we'd only let her."

I gestured for Amelia to hand Flower back to me, which she did. I studied the rodent and with my most patient voice said, "Flower, will you please tell us who is behind all of this?"

"Even if she tells us, how do we know she isn't lying?" Cordelia said.

"We won't know that unless we hear the whole story," I snapped. "Let's hear her out. Give her a chance."

"Fine," Cordelia said, "but every moment we stand here talking is one we won't get back."

I gave Flower a dark look. "Tell us everything."

The possum pawed her whiskers. "I was told I couldn't be sent back to where I'd come from—as the blight, that is. So Snow made me a possum and put me under the crawl space, where I lived for years."

"Twenty," Amelia offered.

"Right." Flower continued. "I lived under the crawl space, but the day of the party, one of the guests spoke to me."

Amelia tapped her foot. "What did he say?"

"She's getting to it," Cordelia snapped.

"Sheesh," Amelia said.

"Go on," I urged.

Flower hesitated. "I was told that I might have an opportunity to get out. That all I would have to do, if asked, was pass on a note."

Flower paused. She glanced down at her paws before looking up and locking gazes with each of us in turn. "I didn't know what I was passing on, but I quickly realized it. After Snow was killed and y'all came to the house. I honestly thought I might be next, that I could be killed as well."

"You're a spirit of blight." Cordelia scoffed. "You can't be killed."

"Being in a flesh-and-blood body makes you think differently sometimes," Flower admitted. "It wasn't rational, but it was a thought. I'm sorry. For all of this. If I hadn't taken the note and given it to you, none of this would ever have happened. And it did. I knew as soon as you started trying to remember the incantation that I would somehow be named. That's why I ran. Not because I'm guilty, but because I was afraid."

Flower hunched her shoulders. "I'm a pawn in this. Same as all of you. We're all pawns, running around trying to stop a magic eater that can't be stopped unless the person who slipped me the paper calls him off."

"Then who was it?" Cordelia spat. "Who gave you the paper and started this mess, and why?"

"I know why they started it," Flower said. "That person was hiding a dark secret. Snow found out. It was only a matter of time before the others discovered it as well. That couldn't happen. The secret couldn't be revealed to the entire town. If it was, then nothing would ever be the same. That person's life in Magnolia Cove would be over."

"How do you know?" I said.

"Because I heard them arguing. That person and Snow." Flower studied each of us in turn. "Before anyone arrived to the meeting, I heard them discussing the situation. Snow accused the person of harnessing power they couldn't control. She pointed out what had happened with the blight, and that the power there couldn't be controlled. Snow said she had covered for that person but was going to stop. There would be no more of a cover-up. She would tell everyone just who had been behind the blight and that Snow was pretty sure the blight wasn't an accident. That person had called down the blight on purpose."

"Why?" Amelia said.

"So the town could suffer and then a few people could step up and be heroes. They were heroes, you know," Flower said. "No matter what you might have heard, they were hailed as saving the town from me. That's what this person wanted. All along."

I frowned. Something seemed fishy. "And Snow was okay with that? I don't understand."

"They were best friends," Flower explained. "Best friends who would never have betrayed each other."

"Then why the betrayal now?" Cordelia asked. "Why would Snow suddenly decide to tell everyone what had happened? That she was covering up for another person?"

Flower rubbed her nose. "Because Snow was dying. She didn't

want people to think that she had been the cause of something so horrible in Magnolia Cove. She was dying of cancer."

"So she would've died anyway," Amelia said sadly.

Flower nodded. "Yes, she would have. But she didn't want to die with that on her conscious."

Cordelia clapped her hands. "Okay. Out with it. Who is it? We can't stand around here all night when there's a dangerous magic eater on the loose. Who is the one who's behind all this?"

Flower's tongue darted out of her mouth as if she were a snake tasting the air. "The person behind everything is—Sylvia Spirits."

We all collectively gasped.

"You're kidding," I said.

Flower shook her head. "I'm not."

"I don't believe it." Cordelia shoved a finger toward the ball. "Not one bit. If you're going to accuse Sylvia Spirits—a person who has tried to keep Magnolia Cove safe for ages—of using us to summon a magic eater, then you'd better have proof."

Flower nodded. "I've got proof. I can show you right now."

TWENTY

"*W*hat is supposed to be at Sylvia's house?" Cordelia asked.

I closed my eyes and knew exactly what Flower was about to mention.

"It's the cap, isn't it? The one that knows all of Sylvia's secrets."

Flower nodded. "She mentioned something about it before the meeting started. Said that soon there would only be one thing that knew her secrets."

"So she suggested that Snow and the others would die?" Amelia said, wide-eyed.

Flower nodded. "Exactly."

"Well, what are we waiting for?" I said. "Let's get out of here and find that cap." I poked the bubble that Flower was still stuck in. "We're not letting you out until we know the truth."

Flower said nothing as Cordelia whisked us from the Cobweb Forest back to town.

We arrived in front of Sylvia's house. "Get us inside, Cordelia," I said.

Cordelia complied, and within a few moments we were tucked safely inside Sylvia's.

I glanced around. "Now where to start looking?"

But before we could begin, the wall in front of us shimmered to life and Betty's head appeared. It was like standing in front of an IMAX version of her head. It was four times its natural size. Basically it looked like someone had plucked Betty's head from her body, pumped it with air and hung it from a string.

Yes, the entire situation was creepy.

"What the heck's going on with y'all?" my grandmother demanded. "I looked for you in the Cobweb Forest and couldn't find one of you. Is that Flower you have?"

Crap. I was hoping we could prove what Flower said before my grandmother tracked us down. No such luck.

"We've got Flower," I said. "We're heading back, but we had a stop to make."

Betty glared at me. "Well get on back to the house. Someone there will tell you where to go next."

"Okay. We'll be along shortly."

She stared at our surroundings. "Are y'all at Syl—"

"Okay, that's fine. We've got to go," I said loudly, hoping my grandmother understood that she wasn't supposed to talk about the fact that it was Sylvia's house.

I really, really hoped she wouldn't say anything. I clapped my hands, and my grandmother's head faded away.

I inhaled a deep breath. "Oh crap. We'd better hurry. There's no telling who all heard her."

"Not to mention she might say something now that the connection's broken," Amelia said.

Cordelia walked past me. "Let's get this over with and find out the truth one way or another."

I looked at the critter. "Where is the hat, Flower?"

The possum shook her head. "I don't know. I just know it's here."

"Well, that should narrow it down," I griped. "Let's start looking."

We searched through the house quickly. It appeared that Sylvia Spirits kept all her hats in—you guessed it—hat boxes in her closet.

"There are some really cool hats in here," Amelia said after pulling a golden one out of a square box. "I wish I could own this many hats."

"People don't run around wearing hats anymore unless you're royal or you're going to church," Cordelia pointed out.

Amelia nodded sadly. "I know. It's a shame."

We opened box after box. A mountain of boxes lay behind us. We'd stripped the closet bare, leaving only clothes hanging like deflated husks of skin on hangers.

I pressed the heels of my hands to my eyes in frustration. "What a waste of time. Just another lie in the sea of lies that has been this entire situation."

Flower nodded toward the very back of the closet. "Wait. There's one more box. That must be it."

Cordelia plucked the box from its spot high on a shelf. I held my breath as she opened the lid. She tipped the bowl toward us.

"Empty," she declared.

I shook my head. "Let's go deliver the possum to them."

"No," Flower shrieked. "It's here."

We started to leave. I reached my hand toward the door when Flower yelled at me, "It's there. The hat. That must be it."

Sitting on a chair, a golden pointed witch's hat gleamed in the lamplight.

"How'd we miss that?" Amelia said.

"We weren't looking for it," Cordelia answered. "We figured it was hidden away."

I moved to the hat. It was gorgeous—a real work of art. Sequins lined the sides, and the shape of it was perfect. Just the sort of hat you'd want for a Halloween party.

My fingers itched to wrap around it. I decided not to stop myself. I plucked it from the chair and smiled. "Wow. This is beautiful."

Cordelia eyed it skeptically. "How does it work?"

"Yeah," Amelia said to Flower. "Now that we have it, how do we make it work?"

The possum shrugged. "How should I know?"

"You're the one who told us about it," Cordelia exploded. "If anyone should know, it should be you."

"Maybe you ask it," the possum offered.

While they were talking, I was mesmerized by the hat. It was truly gorgeous. I brushed my fingertips over the gilded edge. The hat itself seemed to tempt me to put it on, like it was calling me to wear it, but I didn't give in.

We needed to stay focused.

But then a light went on in my head. "I will ask it." I cleared my throat. "Hat, can you tell us about Sylvia Spirits and Snow Wigley? Every part of their relationship?"

My body stiffened in anticipation but nothing happened.

"You probably have to put it on," Amelia suggested.

I swallowed a knot in my throat. "You're probably right." But I was hedging because I could tell the hat had a lot of power—a lot. If I put it on, would I then be able to take it off? Or would I succumb to a force stronger than myself?

I licked my lips.

"I'll do it." Cordelia held open her hand. "I'll put the stupid thing on. Give it to me."

But with all her angst and anger, I thought it was a possibility that those emotions in her would be amplified. That Cordelia wouldn't do well to put on the hat.

"I'll do it," I said. And before anyone had a chance to argue, I plopped the hat on my head.

I was sucked into a whole different world. The question I had asked lingered within the hat. I saw images of Snow and Sylvia when they were much younger, talking.

"This will make us the saviors of Magnolia Cove. We will be heroes," Sylvia was saying.

"By causing a blight?" Snow said in disbelief.

Sylvia reached for her. "By causing it and then removing it from the town. Please, I need you. I can't do this without you."

Snow shook her head. "I don't know."

Sylvia took her hand and squeezed it. "I'll be right beside you. Neither of us will get into trouble. I wouldn't let you take the fall for anything I've done. If something goes wrong, I'll be there to help."

Snow slowly nodded. *"Okay. I'll do it."*

The next image showed the two women in a whirlwind tunnel.

"You have to channel the blight into something," Sylvia was explaining. *"It isn't stable!"*

"But what?" Snow asked.

Sylvia's eyes glittered. *"A familiar."*

The next image was the day of the party. Snow was confronting Sylvia.

"You used me as your pawn. All these years I thought you were good, but you're not. You used me. I will not go to my grave with that knowledge. You will pay for everything you've done."

Sylvia glowered. *"Rethink that."*

"I will not," Snow replied. *"I'll make sure everyone knows it was your fault all that happened."*

Then later, when Snow convinced Flower to help.

"All I need is for you to slip a paper into her pocket. Simple. Can you do it?"

Flower nodded. *"I can."*

The images melted away, and I was left standing wide-eyed in front of my cousins.

"Well?" Amelia said. "Did Sylvia do it?"

My fingers trembled as I removed the hat. "She did. Told Snow that she would regret what she'd done and even pushed Snow to call the blight. She wanted to make it happen, but Sylvia didn't want to be the one who looked guilty."

I shook my head sadly. "How could all this time—how could we have been duped?"

Cordelia glanced sadly at the hat. "I don't know. I feel the same way. That we've been taken advantage of. It's a horrible feeling."

I squeezed her shoulder and looked at her sadly. "We'll make all of this right. If it hadn't been us who summoned the magic eater, Sylvia would've found someone else to do it. This is not your fault."

She nodded. "I'm beginning to understand that, but it doesn't make it any easier to accept."

"Well start accepting it," Amelia said. "Because that's how it is. If you don't accept it, you'll go crazy. You'll always blame yourself, and what good will that do any of us?"

Cordelia snickered. "When did you become all wise and stuff?"

Amelia hiked a shoulder. "I've always been wise; it's just that you don't like to notice or pay attention. I have all kinds of good advice to give. Like for instance, don't let the past keep you from having a future."

I smirked. "That sounds like a refrigerator magnet quote."

Amelia nodded enthusiastically. "It is. Isn't it great?"

"No," I said. "It's cliché and silly."

Amelia's expression fell.

I wrapped an arm around her shoulder. "I'm just kidding. It's awesome. Now," I said sternly. "We need to get out of here. We've got to take this hat and get it to Betty ASAP."

"Agreed," Cordelia said, tucking the hat under her arm. "Let's go."

We headed to the front door, and I was about to open it when a gust of wind blew it open for us.

Leaves and small twigs hit my face. I shielded my eyes, blinded by the gunk filling the atmosphere. I sputtered and spat, spitting out dirt that coated my mouth.

"What the...?" I managed to say before the wind subsided.

The leaves died down. Looming in the doorway stood Sylvia Spirits.

I smoothed the frantic look I knew I had on my face. Had to play this cool. Had to assume that maybe Sylvia didn't know that we knew anything.

"Sylvia," I said quickly. "Thank goodness you're here. My cousins and I had this idea that if we grabbed one of your hats that we'd have the perfect chance to get rid of Erebus."

"Yeah," Amelia took over. "So we came here. We knew that obviously you wouldn't keep the best hats in your store. The most powerful witch's hats you own would be here."

Amelia's gaze darted to Cordelia, who cleared her throat. "Yep. That's right. So here we are. But we didn't find what we were looking for, and we were just about to return to the house. In fact, we were on our way out the door right now."

Sylvia studied each of us in turn. I felt her gaze on me and did my best not to let my emotions take over. I was scared to death. My knees shook and my stomach quivered.

Sylvia was an incredibly powerful witch. I was powerful, too. I was confident in that, but Sylvia also had an advantage.

The hats.

She knew how to use them at will, and that wasn't anything I had mastered.

Sylvia smiled kindly. "Of course. Come now. We need to get to Betty and everyone else if we're going to stop the magic eater. Here." She reached for Flower. "I'll take the possum."

A sick feeling invaded my stomach. It felt like a hundred beetles were crawling around, trying to reach the surface. If I handed Flower over to Sylvia, everything would be lost, I knew that in my gut.

I glanced down at Flower. The little fur ball's eyes glittered with sadness. I dug my fingers into the balloon.

"I'm afraid I can't give her to you. We've got to take Flower to Betty."

Sylvia smirked. "I can help you, Pepper. You can give her to me. We can all go together."

I nodded. "Okay. We can all go together."

Sylvia shook her head. "You know I can't let you leave."

Amelia audibly gulped. "What do you mean? We can all go."

Sylvia shook out her head of red hair. "I know the three of y'all know my secret. I can't let any of you leave. Alive."

TWENTY-ONE

"We don't know what you mean." I shook my head. "We can all go."

Sylvia clapped her hands, and the book of creatures appeared.

Then the other words of the spell clicked into place. *Chained double back and be the twixt, the one who controls you is the mistress.*

Then I understood. Sylvia was the original person who had us summon the creature. Double back. That meant the spell would double back from the blight back to her.

We were so screwed.

Sylvia sneered. "What were you going to do, get me to return Erebus? I'm not the one who summoned him, remember? It was the blight, that little creature right there."

"But you summoned Erebus because you didn't want anyone to know it was your fault," Amelia spat. "You got rid of Snow; why hurt everyone else?"

Sylvia stroked her fingers down the book. "For so long I've kept my secret, and Snow kept it for me, too. But if I was going to get rid of her, I would have to get rid of everyone; otherwise they would suspect that maybe Snow wasn't behind the blight in the first place."

"What?" I scoffed. "Couldn't have your reputation ruined? You helped me. Before—you helped this entire town. Why would you now decide that things are different? That you have to hurt people?"

Sylvia flipped through the book. "Because I have my reputation, and wouldn't it be even greater if the amazing Sylvia Spirits saved the town from a magic eater? A magic eater that I also happen to control?"

She laughed at the looks of surprise on our faces. Her eyes glittered with malice. "Yes, you thought the blight controlled it, but I do. As soon as the magic eater arrived, I worked more magic to control him. He only appears when I need him to."

She rolled her eyes. "That horrible Forbes Henry would already be dead if he hadn't escaped the first time. Really that was a miracle."

"And you escaped," Cordelia said.

Sylvia threw her head back and laughed. "I didn't escape. The creature never appeared."

My stomach twisted. How stupid I'd been. How absolutely completely stupid not to have seen what Sylvia was—someone who lived for themselves and did every selfish thing to help her. She didn't care about Magnolia Cove or any of us—she cared about how she came out in the end after all this.

I felt like I'd been taken for a ride. From the sour expressions on my cousins' faces, I had the feeling they felt the same way.

"So what do we do now?" I said.

"Now we have a moment where the magic eater's brain goes a little haywire and he kills the three of y'all."

The hair on the back of my neck rose. "You wouldn't. We have a history—all of us."

Sylvia shrugged. "It's every woman for herself."

With that, she clapped her hands and a mist appeared in the center of the room. Erebus rose, his twisted face making horror course through my veins.

Sylvia pointed a bloodred fingernail at us. "Take the three women."

I shot a look to my cousins, and that was when all hell broke loose.

I tucked Flower under my arm and the three of us scurried for the door, but Erebus was too fast. The magic eater cut us off. He towered in front of us, his grotesque expression a dark reminder of the horror the magic eater offered.

"The back," I screamed.

We turned to run, but Sylvia slammed the door behind us closed. She cackled. "You can't escape, girls. There is absolutely no way to escape the fate of the magic eater."

I glowered at her sick excitement at our predicament. "You were our friend. You were a friend to Magnolia Cove and to all of us. You lied."

"Yeah," Amelia said. "You spent your entire life lying to us about who you were. That's an absolutely horrible thing to do."

Sylvia shrugged. "Just because I'm a great actress won't save your lives."

"Won't it?" Cordelia shouted.

Her foot lashed out and kicked the book from Sylvia's hands.

"No," Sylvia screamed.

The book flew through the air toward Amelia. "Grab it," Cordelia shouted.

This entire time we hadn't known who'd actually summoned Erebus. Now that we knew, so many other things clicked into place.

The reason why Erebus wouldn't return to the book before was that we didn't know who was controlling him. Only the person controlling him could get him back in the book—pure and simple.

Now we knew who had him, but we also had the book.

"Get that book," Sylvia screamed.

But Erebus had still been commanded to kill the three of us—and he was headed straight for Amelia.

"Let me out of the bubble," Flower shouted. "I can help."

With a single thought I popped the bubble, and Flower scampered across the room and launched herself at Sylvia.

"Throw me the book," I shouted at Amelia.

"Gladly." She tossed it to me, and I caught it in one hand.

Erebus whirled toward me. We had to have enough time to figure out a way to take control back from Sylvia. If we even could.

Right now Sylvia fought off Flower, who was biting at the witch's shoulders.

"Get off me," she shouted.

My brain couldn't work on too many problems at once. The most important obstacle was Erebus and staying alive. As the magic eater closed in on me, I turned to Amelia.

"Catch!"

She nabbed the book from the air. We couldn't keep this game up all night. There was no way. At some point one of us would stumble, and that would be the end.

"Throw the book to me," Cordelia yelled.

Amelia tossed it to her, and Erebus whirled on my cousin. I was about to shout that I was open when Sylvia's voice broke over the chaos.

"That's enough," she yelled.

Everyone stopped, even Erebus. Sylvia stood by the closed front door, claw marks streaking down her cheek, anger flashing in her eyes.

She held Flower by the scruff of her neck. "Y'all thought you could defeat me, really? I've been at this game for too long and have fought too hard for everything to go sour now."

Sylvia extended her free hand to Cordelia. "Now, give me the book and this will all be over quickly. Before you know it, really."

Cordelia hesitated. She glanced at each of us. Amelia seemed not to notice. Instead she opened her backpack and pulled out a mason jar.

It was one of the jars she'd been tasked with cleaning.

It was now spit shined and practically gleaming. "You know, for days now I didn't think these had much power. I didn't think they did anything helpful."

Sylvia glared at Amelia, who continued, unperturbed. "I asked myself why Erasmus Everlasting would make me take them home— why would I have to polish so many of them? It took me a while, but I finally figured out the best way to use them."

"What's this got to do with me?" Sylvia asked.

"Oh," Amelia said, doe-eyed, "it doesn't have anything to do with you. I never thought it did. The only thing this would affect is Flower."

The possum's face lit up. "Me?"

Amelia nodded. "Yep. You. You see, this jar separates things—egg whites from yolks, oil from water—whatever you put inside."

Amelia slowly unscrewed the lid. "But the other thing I'm pretty sure it would separate is a spirit from a body. Like I said, it took me a while to figure that out, but I think it could be done."

Sylvia's eyes widened in horror. "What are you saying? You would release the blight again? You can't do that."

Amelia shrugged innocently. "Can't we? You're trying to kill us with a magic eater, so what other choice do we have?"

"You wouldn't dare," she snapped.

Amelia glanced at Flower. "I think it would be worth the risk, don't you?"

The possum's eyes narrowed. "I think it would definitely be worth the risk. I say we try it."

Sylvia pulled Flower toward her. "No!"

Flower bit the witch on the cheek.

Sylvia dropped the possum. "Ah!" She opened the book. "Erebus, kill them all!"

I was the closest, and the most convenient. The magic eater swept toward me, his mist seeping into my lungs, choking me.

Flower jumped into the mason jar. In a flash of light the possum landed on the floor while a white glow filled the jar. The glowing halo of light zoomed from the jar and encircled Erebus.

I coughed and sputtered, barely noticing that the magic eater was being sucked away from me. His mist receded. My lungs filled with air, and I watched the grim expression on his face transition to one of confusion as the blight zoomed around him like a satellite, yanking Erebus into its own self-made gravitation pull.

"No," Sylvia screamed. "This can't be happening."

I didn't know what was going on. All I knew was that Erebus was being pulled and yanked back, forced to retreat even though he'd been commanded to do the opposite.

Erebus and the blight moved toward Sylvia. Sylvia's eyes widened in horror. The book fell from her hands, landing shut on the floor.

That was when I knew exactly what to do. This was my one chance to stop everything, to end this craziness.

I darted toward the book, flowing around Erebus and the blight. Sylvia didn't notice me. She was too intent on watching the blight come for her.

I madly flipped through the book. "Come on. Where are you?"

Finally I found the page I was looking for and dashed away, putting as much space between the triangle of people and spirits as I could.

I felt Amelia's hand clutch my arm. I shot her a grim look, and she nodded toward the book. Cordelia grabbed Amelia's other arm, and the three of us stood, holding our breath and hoping this nightmare was about to be over.

The blight hooked itself around Sylvia, and the collage of Erebus, Sylvia and blight streamed toward the floor.

"No," Sylvia screamed. "You can't do this! You can't!"

But the blight didn't listen. It pulled with a power like a tornado. As objects fell and shattered around us, the three beings zoomed toward the book until they were sucked into it in a streaming mess of spirit and body.

The white blight, the blackness of Erebus and Sylvia's red hair became a blurred line as the three of them disappeared.

The last bit of Sylvia's voice that I heard was, "No," as she was sucked, screaming, into the pages of the book that she had used to unleash Erebus.

It was fitting, really.

When the last pieces of the three had vanished, the cover snapped shut and silence filled the room.

My cousins and I stood staring at each other. We released our grips and huddled for a hug.

"We did it," Amelia said.

"No, you did," Cordelia corrected. "If it hadn't been for you, we would've all died. All of us, and Sylvia would've gone on to have Erebus destroy our friends and family."

"Well, Forbes Henry isn't exactly my friend," Amelia said.

We laughed. I nodded toward the book. "Don't you think that thing should go to the Vault?"

Amelia nodded. We unlinked our hands, and she picked up the book. "I'll take it over tonight. They have a night deposit I can use."

"Good idea." I glanced at the ground and noticed Flower sitting on her haunches, looking confused. "Cutie??"

Where's CJ? she asked in my head.

Now that she wasn't infiltrated by the blight, she could only communicate with me in her animal way. I opened my arms and picked her up.

"Oh, Cutie, you're in for quite a surprise with CJ."

The door blew open, and Betty, Forbes, CJ and Axel stood on Sylvia's porch, concerned expressions on their faces.

"Where the heck have y'all been?" Betty demanded. "We've been waiting for forever for y'all."

I glanced over at my cousins. The stress of the situation fell off me, and I howled with laughter.

"Well, y'all will never believe what just happened to us. We sent back the blight, Erebus and even caught the person responsible— Sylvia Spirits. They're all trapped in the book."

"] I don't understand," Amelia said. "Why didn't Snow use the book before to trap the blight?"

Betty rubbed her chin. "That may be a question we'll never know the answer to. Perhaps she didn't want to ruin the purity of the book. But anyway, I always thought there was something fishy about Sylvia." She pulled out her pipe and stuck it between her teeth. "Tell us everything."

TWENTY-TWO

"*S*o, do you think maybe we can visit a couple places to get married?"

I nudged Axel from his spot under the hood of his Land Rover. He edged out from under and cleaned the end of the oil dipstick.

"I thought that's what I've been telling you all along?"

I laughed. "You have. But I think now that things have finally calmed down we should be okay to actually spot some places, don't you think?"

He winked at me. "Your wish is my command."

After Sylvia Spirits ended up in the book and the book ended up in the Vault, I showed Garrick the golden hat, which he tucked onto his head and watched the history of what had happened between Snow and Sylvia.

"It's a shame people had to die," he said, "all for one woman's ego."

All of us agreed. It was a grim affair, but there were two funerals to attend—Snow's and Saltz's. Since all this had happened, Betty's words about Snow came out kinder as she understood there was a lot more to who Snow had been than simply a woman who wanted to call a blight and couldn't control it.

One good thing that did come from all of it was that CJ Hix became reunited with Flower, who amazingly hadn't aged a day since she had been used to house the blight.

The reunion between the two brought tears to my eyes.

But with Saltz and Sylvia gone, that meant the Southern School of Magic needed a new headmaster, and it also meant that the hat shop would go up for sale.

Lots of changes occurring in Magnolia Cove. Betty was considering taking over the position of headmistress of the school.

I couldn't blame her for that. But still, I thought it would be better if we let things settle down for a while. Maybe let the dust collect into dust bunnies before we started changing things around.

Which was why I was trying to figure out where Axel and I should get married.

"I think you're right," I said. "We should just do it here. See if we can lower the shields that keep other creatures from entering, invite your family and have a wonderful wedding."

Axel glanced at the sky in relief. "It's about time you agreed with me."

He placed the dipstick back in the oil reservoir and wrapped his arms around my waist. "We could get married atop a pile of dirt and I'd be happy."

I nipped his nose. "I wouldn't be. I'm pretty sure I'm not interested in getting married atop a pile of dirt."

"It's a figure of speech," he argued.

I shot him a teasing look. "Nowhere is that a figure of speech."

"It should be because it means I love you more than anything."

"And I love you."

We kissed and I sank into him, feeling whole and wonderful. Axel was truly my soulmate, and I couldn't wait to be Mrs. Reign. Now all we had to do was set the date.

"How long do you think I need to plan a wedding if we get married here?"

Axel's fingers dug into my back. "A couple of months for folks to clear their schedules, that's about it. The rest of it will require magic, and that's all we'll need. Magic for the dress, the food, the doves that won't poop on anyone's head."

A laugh bubbled in the back of my throat. "So it should be pretty easy."

He nodded. "Yep."

My heart ballooned in my chest. I tipped my chin toward him and leaned in to give Axel another kiss when my phone buzzed in my pocket.

I groaned and unlinked my hands from behind his neck. "Duty calls," he said.

I fished my phone from my pocket. "It's Amelia." I took a step back and answered. "Hello?"

Amelia's voice came clipped. "Hey, don't forget that today's the opening of Southern Wishes."

I groaned. I had completely forgotten. Cordelia and her dad and uncle's store was officially opening. It was the first shop that offered wish granting.

Needless to say, I was totally intrigued. I had to know how the wishes worked.

"The party's tonight, right?"

"It sure is," Amelia said. "You'll want to dress up. Be sure to bring Axel with you."

"Thanks for reminding me."

We said our goodbyes, and I thumbed off the phone. I shot Axel a wide smile. "She was calling to remind me that the wish shop opens tonight."

Axel hiked a perfectly seductive brow. "That's right. I wonder what sort of mischief we can get into with a magic shop in Magnolia Cove?"

I giggled and crossed to him, linking my arm through his. I stretched up to my tiptoes and kissed his mouth. "I don't know," I murmured through kisses. "I wonder what sort of trouble any of us can get into when wishes are possible?"

If I'd only known then what I know now, I never would've questioned the mischief that would happen, because surviving it took just about everything I had.

ALSO BY AMY BOYLES

SERIES READING ORDER

BELLES AND SPELLS MATCHMAKER MYSTERY

DEADLY SPELLS AND A SOUTHERN BELLE

CURSED BRIDES AND ALIBIS

MAGICAL DAMES AND DATING GAMES (November 2019)

SWEET TEA WITCH MYSTERIES

SOUTHERN MAGIC

SOUTHERN SPELLS

SOUTHERN MYTHS

SOUTHERN SORCERY

SOUTHERN CURSES

SOUTHERN KARMA

SOUTHERN MAGIC THANKSGIVING

SOUTHERN MAGIC CHRISTMAS

SOUTHERN POTIONS

SOUTHERN FORTUNES

SOUTHERN HAUNTINGS

SOUTHERN WANDS

SOUTHERN CONJURING

SOUTHERN WISHES (October 2019)

SOUTHERN GHOST WRANGLER MYSTERIES

SOUL FOOD SPIRITS

HONEYSUCKLE HAUNTING

THE GHOST WHO ATE GRITS (Crossover with Pepper and Axel from

Sweet Tea Witches)

BACKWOODS BANSHEE

BLESS YOUR WITCH SERIES

SCARED WITCHLESS

KISS MY WITCH

QUEEN WITCH

QUIT YOUR WITCHIN'

FOR WITCH'S SAKE

DON'T GIVE A WITCH

WITCH MY GRITS

FRIED GREEN WITCH

SOUTHERN WITCHING

Y'ALL WITCHES

HOLD YOUR WITCHES

SOUTHERN SINGLE MOM PARANORMAL MYSTERIES

The Witch's Handbook to Hunting Vampires

The Witch's Handbook to Catching Werewolves

The Witch's Handbook to Trapping Demons

ABOUT THE AUTHOR

Hey, I'm Amy,

I write books for folks who crave laugh-out-loud paranormal mysteries. I help bring humor into readers' lives. I've got a Pharm D in pharmacy, a BA in Creative Writing and a Masters in Life.

And when I'm not writing or chasing around two small children (one of which is four going on thirteen), I can be found antique shopping for a great deal, getting my roots touched up (because that's an every four week job) and figuring out when I can get back to Disney World.

If you're dying to know more about my wacky life, here are three things you don't know about me.

—In college I spent a semester at Marvel Comics working in the X-Men office.

—I worked at Carnegie Hall.

—I grew up in a barbecue restaurant—literally. My parents owned one.

If you want to reach out to me—and I love to hear from readers—you can email me at amyboylesauthor@gmail.com.

Happy reading!

Made in United States
Orlando, FL
19 August 2023

36236932R00102